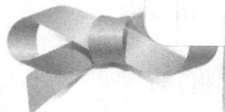

FORBIDDEN LOVE

Spoiled Brats Book Series
Book One
by
Marissa Marchan

FORBIDDEN LOVE

Spoiled Brats Book Series
Book One
Copyright © 2020 by Marissa Marchan

• • ⌘ • •

First Edition: Forbidden Love
ISBN-10: 1701332108
ISBN-13: 978-1701332102
Second Edition: Forbidden Love
ISBN-13: 978-1-953577-08-5 (eBook)
ISBN-13: 978-1-953577-13-9 (Print)
Book Cover Design by Marissa Marchan
Image(s) from Canva
Published by 3 Ways Publishing
https://marissamarchan.com[1]
https://3wayspublishing.wordpress.com[2]

---

1. https://marissamarchan.com/

2. https://3wayspublishing.wordpress.com/

THANK YOU

For the love and support

Leo

Ray-Angelo

Haley-Alexis

Kayla Marie

Lesley-Anne and Hardy

Matt-Derek and Maria

CHAPTER ONE

It was a dark and stormy night. Thunder rattled the window-panes, and powerful gusts of wind slammed the roof. Tom set his open book on the desk, removed his glasses, and rubbed his irritated and sleepy eyes. It was his second book, and he struggled to keep up, since he couldn't understand a word. Tom looked out the window, wondering where his daughter was. He felt as if his mind had split, since he was thinking about so many things simultaneously. Tom had spent the entire night worrying and waiting for the phone to ring. He slumped back in his chair, yawned, and massaged his eyes again with the palm of his hands. Several minutes later, he was pacing and waiting for his daughter to return home.

As his emotions surfaced, he experienced memories of his early childhood. His parents had a small farm, cultivating crops and selling them at local markets. They worked day and night simply to put food on the table. He was just ten years old when he began working on his family's farm, raising cows and pigs to help support his family.

Tom was a dreamer and thinker. He used his talent to gain access to the resources he needed to help him: educational opportunities, scholarships, and grants. He even took odd jobs while at school, such as waiting tables and washing cars. It wasn't only his perseverance that helped him succeed; he never allowed circumstances to impede his achieving the American dream. Through courage, hard work, and determination, Tom rose to become one of the country's most successful and wealthy entrepreneurs.

Then he met his future wife, Martha, one of the most influential women in the advertising industry, at a cocktail party in Hawaii. After only a few months of dating, they married and had twins. They did an outstanding job raising their kids, Jason and TJ, whom they sent to a prestigious school in Beverly Hills, California. And no matter how busy Tom was growing his business empire, he always made time for his children. He was present at their school events and always complimented their talents and abilities.

Tom recalled the day his wife revealed she was expecting their third child. It was the morning of the twins' elementary school graduation. Martha wasn't feeling well, so Tom accompanied her to the doctor. He dropped her off in front of the clinic, before driving around to the rear of the building as he parked his car. He entered the room, and the receptionist, a short, dark-haired lady with spectacles, greeted him with a grin. She informed him that his wife should be out soon. Tom nodded; his gaze fixed on his watch. It was just 10 o'clock, so there was still plenty of time to prepare for the twins' graduation ceremony at 2:00 p.m. To pass the time, he took up a magazine and glanced through the pages without reading a single sentence.

The door slowly opened as the minutes ticked by. An older guy with scruffy gray hair and sagging brows emerged, filling out a report.

"Mr. Grandeville!" shouted the doctor once he recognized Tom. "How have you been?" he asked, smiling.

Tom was taken aback by the doctor's cheerful smile.

"Is everything OK, Dr. Resnick? How is my wife?" he asked, alarmed.

"Your wife is great, Mr. Grandeville. Don't worry," the doctor added, a broad smile on his face.

Tom thought to himself, "There's that smile again."

Martha stepped out of the room. Tom noticed a flush in her cheeks and a glitter in her eyes. She seemed as vibrant as ever, yet there was something different this time. Her conduct piqued his interest. Was he exaggerating? He couldn't be sure. Despite the oddity, he dismissed the notion, believing Martha was simply expressing genuine joy because it was a significant day for them. How often do you get a double triumph when both of your children graduate with honors in a matter of hours?

• • ❧ • •

AT THE GRADUATION CEREMONY, Tom observed his wife was preoccupied and couldn't remain still. She moved around in her seat as if she were on pins. She was concerned with the time, as evidenced by her constant glance at her watch. Martha was acting strangely. When his wife dispatched him and the twins on an errand across town after the ceremony, Tom became suspicious. He couldn't decide how he felt, so he gave her a skeptical look and shuddered, frowning as he glanced at her again. Before he or the twins could ask or say anything, Martha jumped into a waiting taxi on the curb and waved as it drove away. Perplexed, Tom and the twins were still standing where she had left them.

Tom got irritated and suspicious, but he didn't want his children to know how he felt. He laughed as he rubbed his chin.

"Your mother is throwing a lavish celebration for you two. It's clear she's trying to get rid of us."

"What's with the secrecy? It's not like we don't know about our party," Jason added, scratching his head in puzzlement.

"Well, you know your mother. She enjoys arranging things and may be rather sneaky." Tom feigned a laugh.

TJ frowned. "Why not tell us instead of sending us away? She never even let us change our clothing. For God's sake, we're still dressed in our caps and gowns."

"It's vital to your mother, boys. She wouldn't have asked us to do this if she didn't need us to. Let's leave it at that, OK?" remarked Tom, putting on a phony smile. The truth was that something was worrying him. Something serious happened to his wife, and he did not know what to do. He planned to talk to her after the party, but for the time being, he had to put on a cheerful face in front of the twins.

"Okay, Dad, but how long are we supposed to be gone?" TJ asked.

"Your mother will not go to this trouble merely for us to return right away. Let's go to the store. You can help me pick a new fishing rod."

The father and sons spent a long time in the mall and ended up buying things they didn't need. They were back on the road, heading home after a few hours. The number of automobiles parked in the driveway astounded them. It was fully occupied.

"Wow! Did Mom invite the entire neighborhood?" asked the twins, laughing.

When they entered the house, their guests greeted them with warm hugs. Tom glanced around, wondering what God's name had compelled his wife to decorate in such garish hues that were inappropriate for their children's graduation celebration.

What the hell is going on? What was she thinking? he murmured. He was slow to catch on and sought to decode the enormous hints Martha left around the house.

"Pink and blue pattern; my goodness!" he said, his irritation audible.

Meanwhile, the twins were taken aback by the scene in front of them. They thought their mother had lost her usual knack for creativity. Jason tripped over his own feet and fell flat on his face because he wasn't paying attention to where he was going. While they were busy drinking champagne and chatting, the guests expressed their anxiety, a look of concern on their faces as they shared their fears.

"Jason, what happened? Are you OK?" the guests questioned him, grabbing his outstretched hands and pulling him to his feet.

Jason was too confused. He hadn't expected to embarrass himself in front of everyone at his party. Jason, as charming as he was, rose up and beamed at everyone.

"Nothing's wrong with me. Don't worry," Jason remarked as he wiped dirt and dust from his trousers.

He looked around and scratched his head in disbelief. His mother produced an enthralling party environment. Rainbow origami cubes and multi-colored crepe paper streamers hung from the ceiling. On the table, there was a pink and blue balloon background, matching tablecloths, and coordinated napkins and plates. The centerpiece was an enormous strawberry vanilla cake with pink and blue icing, and the words 'Will we celebrate in pink or blue?' written on it.

"What's going on, Mom?" Embarrassed, the twins asked. Pink was not a favorite hue of theirs.

"Yeah, Martha, what in the name of God is going on?" Tom protested. "What's the matter with you?"

Martha looks stunning in her peach floral dress, laughing and smiling. As she stepped center stage, she looked radiant, and Tom's suspicion transformed to surprise when his wife spoke.

"We appreciate your presence tonight for this joyous event. We should share this excitement with friends and family while we are celebrating not one, but two occasions. Guess what? I'm pregnant!"

A loud applause rang across the house, as a deafening roar of voices praised Martha from every corner of the room. They raised their glasses in salute, perhaps a bit too freely as the wine flowed. It was a fantastic event, and everyone had a great time. It was the most amazing night they'd ever had!

When he felt his wife's arms around him, Tom snapped back to the present. Martha had entered the study room without his notice.

"Tom!" Martha smiled; her gaze fixed on him.

"I'm sorry, darling. Did you say something?" he asked, attempting to regain his composure.

"Go to bed, Tom. Don't worry. I still have some knitting to do. I'll sit in my favorite chair by the window and wait for our daughter," Martha remarked, smiling.

Before nodding, Tom took a minute to gaze at his lovely wife's face.

"Yes, honey," he crooned as he leaned down and kissed his wife on the cheek, before saying goodnight and retiring upstairs to sleep.

Martha was knitting in her cozy chair when she became apprehensive after hearing a faint rumble of thunder. She stared out the window, but all she saw was lightning flashing all the time. She thought how disrespectful her daughter was for not calling them. The storm's rain pounded on the window. Martha sat up all night, worried and staring out the window, waiting for her daughter to come home.

As the minutes passed, Martha's turn came to have a flashback when she found out she was pregnant with her daughter. It was the most joyous day of her life. It was the morning of the twin's graduation from elementary school. She went to see her family doctor since she was feeling ill. They had done the blood work a few days before. Martha couldn't believe it when her test results came back and her doctor informed her she was six weeks pregnant. She was at a loss for words. She and Tom had always wanted another child, but it had never happened. And now it's happened. Martha requested Dr. Resnick not inform her husband of the pregnancy. She wanted to surprise her family, and the twins' party was the ideal place and time to do it. She pledged to make it an occasion to remember for everyone.

Martha was nervous and couldn't stay seated throughout the graduation ceremony. She continually excused herself to go to the restroom, but in reality, she was making phone calls to organize and arrange the party. As soon as the ceremony was over, Martha sent Tom and the boys on an errand to keep them out of the house for a few hours. Martha jumped into a waiting taxi she had called earlier, and she kept waving at her husband and children until the cab pulled away.

The party planner and her team worked tirelessly to set up the decor, a food table, and party favors at several stations. Martha didn't believe she could pull it off with such short notice, but it was amazing what you could carry out when money was not an issue.

The guests arrived. They recovered from the first shock with a sudden intake of breath, and took in the unexpected sight of the bizarre decorations around the house. As Tom and the twins entered the room, they were taken aback. That was something Martha expected.

When she revealed her pregnancy, Jason and TJ were the first to respond. They screamed at the top of their lungs. While everyone else shouted, cheered, and congratulated them, it startled Tom into silence. It took him a while to grasp what she had said. Tom beamed with joy until he could not contain his happiness and screamed at the top of his lungs, "Yahoo!"

Martha sighed as she returned to the present.

What have I done?

She admitted spoiling her daughter and pampering her since she was born. She and Tom were always there to comfort her when she cried. When their schedule grew too hectic, they hired a wonderful nanny to look after Vanessa. Their daughter grew worse when she learned to walk, wreaking havoc wherever she went. Nanny Maureen had to trail her around all day. She only stayed with the Grandeville for a year, before leaving to work for another rich family.

Vanessa had transformed into a monster when she was four years old, and she had gotten away with terrible things for far too long. She played rough and knocked over a few priceless vases around the house. To keep up with her, her parents had to employ two nannies. Martha catered to her every need to prevent her inevitable outbursts. Vanessa had to have anything she desired. Martha was angry with herself. Instead of allowing her daughter to be disappointed, she paved the way for Vanessa to have a pleasant life.

Her thoughts were interrupted as she heard a vehicle pull into the driveway. Martha rose from her chair, walked over to the window, and peered through the blinds. She breathed a sigh of relief when she saw her daughter's Mercedes-Benz come to a halt. Vanessa reappeared shortly afterwards, carrying two Gucci shopping bags.

"Hi Mom! What a wonderful day I spent with my friends. I'll see you in the morning," Vanessa muttered as she headed upstairs to her room, leaving her poor mother shaking her head in disbelief at raising such an immature daughter.

CHAPTER TWO

Vanessa Florence Grandeville, or "Ness," as her parents nicknamed her, was a bright young lady with a spoiled disposition. Why wouldn't she be? She was born to a wealthy family from the Southern California suburbs, where many of the homes were custom-built in an exclusive gated community. Vanessa, the youngest of three children, was born with the proverbial silver spoon in her mouth. She grew up on the family estate in Beverly Hills, where she attended one of the country's most prestigious private schools.

While most parents tried to teach their children to appreciate what they had, Martha and Tom wanted Vanessa to feel special. They overindulged her, giving her everything she desired: money, material belongings, and even rewards with no expectations for her fulfilling any obligations. They did not educate their daughter to be grateful for everything she had. Vanessa knew well that her parents and brothers adored her, and she took advantage of this to get their attention. She went from being the loveliest girl in the world when she wanted something to being a monster in seconds when she didn't get her way. She grew up without restrictions or supervision.

For Tom and Martha, they believed there was nothing wrong with how they raised their daughter, so Vanessa took everything for granted. She learned to get away with things without having to face the repercussions of her conduct. Vanessa looked down on the less fortunate. She grew up spoiled, believing she deserved special attention everywhere she went.

Vanessa was twelve years old when she was invited to attend a sleepover party at a friend's vacation home in Santa Barbara for the weekend. It was Esmeralda's thirteenth birthday. Her parents organized an all-day and all-night event for Esmeralda and her friends, including a picnic, sports, fishing, and a slumber party. They allowed parents to stay, but the children's overnight was in another section of the house, preventing them from checking on the youngsters. It was one of Esmeralda's stringent party regulations. Vanessa was delighted to go, since several of her school classmates would be there.

Tom had just returned home from the office when he heard his daughter having a loud argument with her mother in the kitchen.

"Mom, I'm twelve years old. I'm big enough to go!" Vanessa was voicing her displeasure.

"What is this?" asked Tom as he entered and kissed his wife.

"They invited your daughter to a sleepover party in Santa Barbara this weekend, and I told her she couldn't attend."

Vanessa yelled.

"Dad, tell Mom I'm old enough to go to a sleepover party. Mom is just too paranoid."

"Don't talk like that, young lady," Martha said emphatically.

"What happened to my beloved parents? The greatest parents in the world?" Vanessa asked, putting on her best sweet-sounding act as tears streamed down her cheeks.

"Don't look at me, honey," Tom murmured as he lifted his hands in the air. "It's still up to your mother."

"Tom, it's an overnight party," Martha responded. "She's not even a teen yet."

"Oh, Mom," Vanessa said. "I'm old enough to go!" she screamed at the top of her lungs, stomped her feet, and burst into tears.

The image of her daughter sobbing broke Tom's heart into a million pieces. "Oh, please don't weep, honey. You know how much I despise seeing you in this state. Okay, I'll speak with your mother."

Vanessa grinned for a moment, then grimaced. When she saw her mother would not budge from her decision to let her go, she wailed and complained until her parents would do almost anything to get her to stop. They gave in to their daughter's demand, and Vanessa got her way again, but she disliked the thought of her father accompanying her to the party.

· · ৵৵ · ·

IT WAS A WONDERFUL sunny day. Tom had a business conference in Oxnard scheduled for the weekend, so Martha had to take their daughter to the party. Vanessa packed her beauty kit and nail polish, although the invitation stated not to.

"Did we forget anything?" As they climbed into the car, Martha asked Vanessa for the second time.

"Positive, Mom. Picnics and sports are out of the question. I've got everything I need for the party in this small cosmetic bag," Vanessa informed her mother.

Martha gave her daughter a doubtful glance and scoffed at her before turning away.

"All right, let's go," Martha said, as she motioned for the driver to go.

When they arrived at the party, a few members of their social circle greeted them, including Elizabeth, Esmeralda's mother.

"Hello, Vanessa. I'm delighted you made it," Esmeralda smiled.

Vanessa glanced up, surprised. She hadn't expected Esmeralda to welcome her guests when they arrived. She hid her cosmetic bag in one of her large bags, but Esmeralda was quick to notice it.

"What do you have there?" she asked.

Vanessa blinked at Esmeralda. "I'm sorry, I was just putting away my wallet."

Esmeralda gazed at her. She opened the bag without uttering a word.

"Humph! And what is this? I told you we'd supply everything we needed for our slumber party!"

Esmeralda took the cosmetic kit and walked away.

Vanessa was enraged, but she tried hard to calm down. She couldn't say anything to Esmeralda. She could send her home. It was her party, and Vanessa wanted to stay for the sleepover. Otherwise, if she was the only one not there, everyone at school would label her a loser. Everyone had been talking about Esmeralda's famed sleepover party for a long time. It was the closest thing to freedom they could get: telling stupid jokes, getting makeovers, and talking about boys. Vanessa reminded herself not to invite Esmeralda to her glitzy thirteenth birthday party, which was coming up in two months.

The first event of the day was a family fishing tournament. It was summer, and the lake was teeming with fish such as trout, salmon, catfish, and black bass. They could find a few around the docks or along most of the lake's shoreline. Elizabeth would name the winner based on the weight of all the fish caught. She would donate $10,000 to the grand prize winner's school or a charity of the winner's choice.

A few people forgot to bring their fishing gear. Fortunately, the hosts had many spares ready to lend. Meanwhile, Martha was on the phone with Tom when she noticed the invitation card on the table that said, "Bring Your Fishing Gear."

When Martha searched for Vanessa, she was enraged. She found her sitting under a large shade tree, listening to music on her iPod.

"Didn't I ask you earlier if there was anything we needed to bring, and you replied no? Look at what you've done! We are the only family not taking part in the competition," she retorted.

"I have no plans to go fishing, Mom. I don't want to get soaked."

Martha shook her head in frustration, unable to believe what her daughter had just said. Vanessa could see how upset her mother was, but she shrugged and didn't even apologize. She put her headphones back on and sang along with the song.

Moments later, Vanessa heard a commotion on the lake and saw her pals swoon over a cute guy with curly, long blond hair. She recognized him. Ted was Esmeralda's fifteen-year-old cousin. He was out fishing with his father. Vanessa noticed her classmates rush to get their fishing rods ready to join him. Ted appeared to enjoy the attention he received from them. She grew envious. Vanessa got up and went to join them. When Ted ignored Vanessa, she insisted she be given a fishing rod, but there was none available. Everyone was having so much fun that they didn't want Vanessa to use theirs.

Vanessa was enraged. She took out her phone and dialed their driver's number, who was at home enjoying breakfast with his family because it was his day off. He dropped Vanessa and her mother off early that morning, and was not scheduled to pick them up again until the next day.

"I want you to go home and get me my fishing pole!"

"But, miss, I'm at home with my family. I'm going the opposite way, and it will take me nearly a full day to travel to your house, pick up the fishing rod, and then bring it to you."

Vanessa yelled.

"I don't care. Bring my fishing rod right now!" She was much more raucous this time. "I need my fishing pole! My father will fire you if you don't deliver it right away!"

Vanessa did not know that everyone was listening to her, and they couldn't stop laughing at her foolish conduct. Martha was so ashamed of her daughter's performance that she sought to hide her face.

Meanwhile, the driver was trembling and hadn't finished his meal. He returned to Grandeville's house to get the fishing rod. He was traveling so fast that he almost collided with the automobiles in front of him.

• • ⌘ • •

A CAR PULLED UP IN the driveway two hours later. It was Tom, with a brand-new fishing pole in his hand. Martha approached him and asked why he was there.

"Our butler contacted me in the middle of my meeting to inform me that our driver had suffered a slight stroke. Roger is currently recuperating in the hospital. I spoke with the doctor on the phone, and he assured me he would be OK. He was simply stressed. Do I bother to inquire why?" asked Tom, his gaze fixed on his daughter.

"Hello, Dad. How are you doing? When did you arrive?" Vanessa asked as she yanked on his arm. "Come on, Dad. Let me show you around."

"Vanessa, the butler informed me that you insisted Roger bring you the fishing rod. Didn't you realize today was his day off? You should've brought it with you when you left the house."

Tom sat with his arms folded across his chest, waiting for his daughter to say anything. When Martha intervened and told him it was too late to enter the tournament, Tom felt enraged.

"They admitted Roger to the hospital. I had to leave in the middle of my meeting to stop at the store on the way here to buy this fishing rod, and for what?"

It was the first time Vanessa had seen her father furious with her. She stayed mute, in fact. Vanessa didn't want to draw any more attention to herself, as everyone turned to listen in on their heated conversation. She lowered her head and looked down at her feet. She averted her gaze, then returned it with a grin to her father.

"Vanessa, dear, demonstrates empathy for people's sentiments," her father remarked in a clear, soft voice. "Roger had a nervous breakdown because of his anxiety. He was concerned about losing his job. Nobody deserves to be treated like that.

Do you get what I'm saying, Vanessa?" Tom stated as he took a bottle of water and cleared his throat.

Vanessa merely nodded yes while standing there in silence, and then she burst into tears. She apologized as she sobbed, tears streaming from her eyes and landing on her cheek. Every word Vanessa spoke warmed Tom's heart. His rage had faded. He wrapped his arm around her and hugged her tightly.

"I knew you'd get it."

"I'm sorry, Dad. I didn't intend for Roger to..." She paused. Her eyes welled up with tears again. "Everyone else is having a fantastic time fishing, but I'm not. All I wanted was my fishing pole so I could join them."

Tom grinned and extended his arm to her again.

"Oh, don't weep, dear. You've learned your lesson. That's all I'm asking. Please be mindful of other people's feelings, OK?"

"All right, Dad," she murmured, brushing her tears away.

Martha joined the father and daughter in their embrace. Everyone, including Ted, witnessed the event from a distance, and his face fell into a stunned expression.

"That selfish brat can get away with anything. She is one of the most spoiled brats on the planet. How come they can't see she's simply playing them?" he asked.

Esmeralda and her companions agreed with a shrug of their shoulders.

While Tom was consoling Vanessa, Elizabeth drew Martha aside and pushed her to seek help.

"It's normal for us to want to give our children everything we have, but Martha, you're raising a tyrant. Remember the old saying about spoiled rotten kids growing up to be spoiled rotten adults? Your daughter will grow up thinking everything should be handed to her on a silver platter. If your daughter does not get what she wants, she may have a tantrum. Wake up, Martha, before it's too late," Elizabeth said.

Martha knew Elizabeth was right, but she couldn't face hurting Vanessa.

My daughter just needs attention to behave. She'll be all right. Martha said, trying to convince herself.

CHAPTER THREE

Vanessa, now a teenager, grew more attractive with time—so gorgeous that everyone forgot how spoiled she was. When she wore a sleeveless sundress on a warm, bright day, her beauty shone through. Vanessa delighted in showing off her physique on the beach. She reveled in the limelight. Vanessa was the same Vanessa she had been from childhood, with little regard for other people's sentiments. Many males wanted to date her, but they soon discovered she was incredibly high maintenance. She always expected the red-carpet treatment, and if no one could give her what she wanted, she told them to take a walk.

Vanessa and her privileged friends all hailed from wealthy families: Rachel, Stephanie, Jennifer, Alexandra, and Samantha ruled Beverly Hills Prep Academy. They were known as Spoiled Brat Princesses, or SBPs, because they were superficial, gorgeous, and popular, and they had no issue displaying their wealth and luxurious lifestyles. They mocked the nerdy-looking people, but many envied them.

Their friendship began in eighth grade, when they went on a field trip to New York City.

Under the direction of their two art instructors, twelve eighth grade students traveled on a two-day, fun-filled educational trip to New York City, home to world-class museums. Their agenda included visits to art galleries and exhibitions,

Broadway shows, and historic structures and landmarks. Other attractions include the Botanical Garden, planetariums, and historical excursions. These were the recommendations of the professors, but the students had varied opinions about what they thought was fun. They opted to visit Keansburg Amusement Park, horseback riding, and view the famed outdoor skating rink in Central Park.

The parties checked into their five allotted rooms at the prestigious Majestic Inn Hotel. The teachers divided the students into four groups of three and assigned them rooms, with the teachers sharing the last one. But the affluent teens, believing they were superior to other cliques, refused to share a room with anyone.

In a fit of anger, the teachers crammed them all into a single room. All six of them to teach them a lesson. The instructors requested extra rollaway beds be brought into the room. The youths objected, claiming they didn't enjoy sharing, but the teachers demanded they stay together or sleep in the corridor, which made them cringe. The youngsters shared an overcrowded room, since they didn't have a choice.

As expected, each of the schoolgirls lacked social skills and didn't know how to get along with others.

"You are not the center of the universe," Vanessa snarled as she slammed the door behind her.

"You are not my mother to tell me what I can and cannot do," Jennifer protested.

When the other four joined in, the squabble erupted into a yelling war, with one even threatening to call the teachers.

"If you do that, we'll sleep in the hallway!" Stephanie reminded everyone.

The violent yelling session between the females concluded after an hour of fierce arguments and nasty disputes over everything. The adolescents spoke and discovered their similarities and differences. Because they were all in the same room, the friendships they formed were tremendous. They struck an instant bond, as if they had known each other in another's life. What piqued their interest the most was the fact that they shared a favorite pastime: shopping!

When the trip was over, the girls remained the best of friends. They shared their happiness and sorrows, and they supported one another through challenging trials, difficulties, high school, and boys. They were always at each other's sides and became part of their families.

· · ❦ · ·

IN THEIR SENIOR YEAR of high school, the SBPs had always taken pleasure in being the focus of attention. They threw parties for their friends to show off their wealth. Vanessa stayed in a suite at one of her family's Grandeville holiday resorts. Sometimes the party was planned as a little get-together for her female friends, but it got out of hand when many individuals showed up uninvited. When the party was over, there was filth everywhere. They trashed the place, leaving garbage everywhere. The property management and employees were used to Vanessa's antics, so they turned a blind eye and hired an outside cleaning company to restore the damage to the room. The one thing they were grateful for was that Vanessa never permitted drinking or smoking on their property.

Vanessa once invited the SBPs to her mansion after school. She had a new CD that she wanted her friends to hear. Carmen, her cook, spent a long time making her excellent spaghetti for her pals. Vanessa stared at it as she placed it on the table and sighed, telling Carmen to prepare something else.

"Vanessa, spaghetti is my favorite." Rachel said, with her mouth full. "It tastes fantastic!"

"Yeah, Vanessa. You should try it," Samantha said, wiping her lips with a delicate white handkerchief.

Vanessa scowled as she refused to eat the spaghetti, but her pals insisted, so she took a taste. Her buddies were correct. Carmen did an outstanding job. The spaghetti was excellent—better than the cake or ice cream she had intended to eat—but her pride got in the way, and she told her friends she still didn't like it. Vanessa sent Carmen back to the kitchen to make something different. The cook was unhappy, since she had cooked the pasta for Vanessa. She crept back into the kitchen and offered the girls cake and ice cream.

"Vanessa, you're too much. I know you enjoyed the spaghetti. I could tell by the look on your face. Carmen is a fantastic chef. Why do you have to be so difficult?" Jennifer asked.

"I'll tell you why—because I can!" she said. She beamed, and her friends returned her smile as they exchanged high-fives.

There were several examples of pampered children squandering educational chances and wasting their parents' fortune. Vanessa was not one of them—it was the one nice quality she possessed. In truth, she had a good brain, was brilliant, and had always done well in school. She was knowledgeable about their family's affairs, but had no role in their business.

"Why should I do anything?" she questioned her friends, who, of course, invariably agreed with her.

During Career Day at Beverly Hills Prep Academy, a high-fashion model agency dropped by. Everyone wanted to be a famous fashion model, so the students went crazy. All the aspiring models accepted the agent's business card, hoping to become the next supermodel. Meanwhile, the SBPs sat in the shade of a tree, observing everyone else's folly. It didn't pique their curiosity about discovering what Career Day may have given them. Why should they? They would have inherited millions from their parents, eventually. So why would they work?

"Did you hear what I said?" Jennifer asked, fighting to recover her breath after returning from prowling about the campus. "A high-fashion model agent is giving a lecture in the assembly hall at school. Everyone is raving about her, and they are attempting to get her business card, hoping to get an interview."

"Why would anyone want to exploit their bodies? For money? Fame? What?" Vanessa asked.

"I'm not sure, but all I know is that everyone is in a state of panic over this. Everyone, and I mean everyone, in the school wants to be a model," Jennifer explained.

"Well, not everyone. I'm uninterested. Steph, are you? Rachel, how about you? Sam? Alex?" Vanessa asked.

"It makes no difference whether we're interested. Because we're merely sitting here, the agent is unaware of our existence. People might have thought we were not good enough to be models. We must maintain our status. We have to show the agent that we are better than everybody else," Jennifer explained.

"If you want to be models to prove something, I'm all for that. Let's march into the assembly hall and meet the agent," Samantha said.

"Count me in!" Rachel said.

"Okay then, we all agree. We'll be high-end fashion models," Vanessa said.

The females laughed and gave each other high-fives. Alexandra stopped them as they were ready to proceed towards the assembly hall.

"Wait a second. We don't need a stinking, second-rate Los Angeles agent. You seem to forget that my father socializes with New York City's fashion elite. We're headed straight to New York. Just leave everything to me," she murmured, her eyes twinkling.

"Oh, my goodness, Alex," Rachel said. "We had forgotten about it. So, we'll leave everything to you."

"Yes, leave everything to me. I'll take care of it," Alexandra said.

The SBPs disliked being fashion models, but it was the "in" thing to do at the time, since everyone was obsessed with it. They had to show that SBPs were the best.

Vanessa didn't want anyone to overshadow her. She approached her parents, believing they had more fashion contacts than Alexandra's father. Her parents disapproved of the news that she intended to be a model.

"I enjoy the finer things in life, such as clothes, shoes, automobiles, and jewelry, and I will not settle for anything less!" Vanessa screamed and threw a fit. She was completely out of control.

Her parents knew well that this was one of her dramatic outbursts to get what she desired. They opposed their daughter's professional decision and suggested she get a doctorate or law degree. Her parents forbade her from pursuing modeling, but Vanessa insisted.

"Given our fortune, we expect you to follow in your brothers' footsteps and assist with the family business, or pursue a career as a doctor or lawyer. We expect you will open your own clinic or law firm, rather than work as a fashion model."

"No!" Vanessa screamed.

"Vanessa, relax!" Her father said as he hugged her.

"No!" Vanessa shouted again. She snatched herself from her father's embrace and erupted in wrath.

"Vanessa, please stop!" her mother said.

Vanessa fidgeted for a split second. She would not allow her parents to impede her ambitions or whatever she was trying to do. Despite their protestations, Vanessa delivered her portfolio to Alexandra, whose father had connections in the New York modeling industry.

A few weeks later, Vanessa and her fellow SBPs received letters from the modeling agency welcoming them. There was a shouting match at Vanessa's house, but her parents surrendered to avoid additional squabbles, but with conditions. Vanessa agreed to make a concession. Vanessa planned to move to New York as soon as she finished high school, which was just a month away, to follow her ambition of being a fashion model, but she had to return home after a year to attend college. They would not oppose it more if she still wanted to return to New York after that.

When word got out that the SBP's first fashion engagement was in New York City, it became the talk of the school. Everyone envied them, which made the SBPs more pompous and arrogant than before.

. . ⚮ . .

TIME QUICKLY PASSED. Vanessa and her friends wasted no time. They moved to New York as soon as they graduated from high school. Possessing connections with powerful people, as well as having amazing knockout looks and a killer physique, helped. During New York Fashion Week, Vanessa and her friends strutted down the runway. Vanessa quickly realized, however, that the moment did not measure up to her expectations. Beyond the glamour and dazzle of the runway shows were the hectic schedules of the models. The casting, the fittings to decide what clothes to wear, hair, makeup, interviews, and off-site shows, not to mention sleeping in a room with five or six other exhausted models—models who thought it was unfair Vanessa and her friends were accepted so easily, while they had to work so hard to get a spot on the runway. Other models were resentful, and it harmed the situation when Vanessa and her friends acted like Divas all the time.

Vanessa couldn't stand the sound of the shouting uproar, back-and-forth ranting, and too much drama going on backstage, and decided it was time to go home.

"I don't need this ridiculous and convoluted existence, even if it means fame and fortune. You are welcome to it!" Vanessa addressed the envious models. She collected her belongings and marched out the door, not looking back. She headed for the door on her way back home with her friends behind her.

The mouths of the envious models dropped open. Nobody ever walked away from fame. As they saw the SBPs go out and slam the door behind them, it stunned them into silence.

CHAPTER FOUR

I t was the early hours of a spring morning along the coast of Towi, a small island in the Pacific Ocean. You could only get there by boat or private helicopter. Unlike the other adjacent islands, Towi Island remained one of the world's most segregated communities. Its residents liked the quiet tranquility and the wonderful, picturesque setting like no other. They rejected initiatives to encourage tourism. Towi Island had a restricted number of hotel rooms, but it was large enough to host fifty tourists. Bicycles were the primary mode of mobility in the township, but a few people still drove.

Towi Island, home to nearly 5,000 full-time residents, was primarily a fishing town and the home of many fishermen. It boasted an abundance of fresh seafood and locally produced vegetables, not to mention crystal-clear seawater, where children and adults could swim, fish, and play confidently in the ocean. It was a calm and welcoming environment where everyone knew everything about everyone else.

As the rest of the world rested, twenty-three-year-old Michael, a kind-hearted and gorgeous young fisherman with a suntanned face, was busy putting together the sailboat and his gear to set sail for the best catch. The weather prediction for the day was favorable.

Michael's father was a fisherman, as was his father's father before him. At his father's behest, he became a fisherman and an aspiring cook by choice. Through his remarkable gifts of confidence, knowledge, and wit, Michael successfully became an expert fisherman and learned to appreciate deep-sea fishing. He loved being in the ocean. After all, it was in his blood.

Michael was five years old the first time he saw his father clean his tackle box and fishing gear before retiring to bed. He always enjoyed how they gleamed in the morning when the light glinted across the sea. When his father set sail, he wanted to join him, but his mother insists he stay on shore since he was too young. Michael waved to his father and waited for him at the pier till he returned home, a sorrowful expression on his face.

When Michael turned eleven, his mother decided he was old enough to go fishing with his father. His dad taught him the art and joy of fishing. His father was happy about him showing interest, because Michael awoke earlier than he did, eager to arrange the fishing equipment and gear. Michael learned to bait the lines with herring and experienced the excitement of capturing his first fish. His father taught him how to go spearfishing. Michael learned how to navigate the boat and safely return it to port. He gained a lot of knowledge from his father, whether it was fishing skills or weather, but most importantly, he taught him how to be a better person.

Michael was an active youngster who played sports when he wasn't fishing with his father. He relished every minute of his Little League baseball games in the blazing heat of July. Michael began kayaking at twelve, and as an adult, he was an active and longtime member of the Towi Canoe Club, taking part in many events and contests. He was the finest, if not the greatest, player in their town. Michael was a wonderful son who was well-liked by everyone. His parents were proud of him.

Michael had come to terms with the notion that life was unpredictable and harsh. He lost his mother while he was a sophomore in high school, and his father died two years later. He struggled to believe he was now alone, but not a day went by that he didn't think about or miss them. Fortunately for him, his parents left him a house, a sizable inheritance in the bank, a fishing boat, and a vintage 1951 Chevrolet 3100 truck that his father won in a lottery many years ago.

Michael awoke at around 3 a.m. every day. He ate breakfast, gathered his belongings, dressed warmly, and left his house. Michael met his fellow fishermen and spent most of the morning at sea. He sometimes returned with barrels full of fish, and other times he only returned with a half-full barrel. Michael enjoyed fishing, and even when he was alone on the boat, he hummed a melody like his father did when they went fishing together. It made him feel as though his father was still there with him and had never left. At the end of his fishing trip, he would hang his nets to dry, pick up trash, and fix any holes that had formed. Then he looked after his goats, pigs, and chickens. Michael planted vegetables in a medium-sized garden. He started preparing his meal, and it wouldn't be complete without fish or seafood. Michael whipped up a fantastic salad, using his freshly picked vegetables from the garden and a homemade vinaigrette that had the perfect zesty Dijon bite. Great cooking came easily to him.

Every month, Michael and the people of the village held their typical Hawaiian celebration feast, which was accompanied by entertainment such as dancing, playing games, and singing. Michael always had an enjoyable time with his friends, whom he considered his family. But when he was alone, he missed his father. His favorite pastime was strolling down the pier, watching the waves lapping against the rocky beach. Michael recalled a certain occasion with his father when he first taught him how to fish in the lake. He was overjoyed, but he thought it thrilled his father more than he was. Michael grinned as his thoughts wandered back to that day at the lake, when he caught his first fish.

Do you think they'll bite, Dad?

Yes, son, I am certain.

That's what he appreciated about his father. He never discouraged him from trying. His father's eyes twinkled with pleasure at his son's accomplishments.

Dad, I got a bite!

It's a big one! Take it easy, son. Keep the line tight. Allow him to exhaust himself before you attempt to bring him in.

Michael exuded confidence. It was his first catch. After a few minutes of fighting the fish, he pulled it into the boat, where his father grabbed it by the lower jaw and hauled it out of the water.

Look at that beauty! His father said, while Michael jumped up and down with delight.

Dad, I've got a big one!

Yes, you did, son. Someday, you'll be a terrific fisherman. Remember, son, to be proud of your heritage. If you learn about the ocean, you will reap its rewards. Remember that when I am no longer here in this world, just look out at the wide sea and I'll be watching you. Remember that, Michael.

The memories of his father always brought chilling goose-bumps to his skin and tears to his eyes. He missed his father. If only he could turn back the clock. If only...

.. ⚘ ..

MICHAEL GREW UP LOOKING like he belonged to GQ magazine. Teen girls and ladies swooned over him because he was six-feet-two-inches tall, had sun-streaked surfer's hair, and had magnificent eight-pack abs. Michael possessed an irresistible charisma that drew you in without you even realizing it, but he had no intention of courting any of them. Raul was also perplexed.

Raul, his cousin and childhood best friend, was the total opposite of Michael. He possessed a gigantic ego the size of Jupiter and was a notorious womanizer, often bragging about the women he dated. Raul, like Michael, was attractive, standing five feet nine inches tall, and sporting short, wavy, black hair. He enjoyed being the center of attention at parties. Raul dominated most talks, which always revolved around the same two topics: him and women. He encouraged Michael to join him several times, but Michael always declined, claiming he was too busy.

"You can't work 24 hours a day, seven days a week. It's not good for you," Raul added.

"I enjoy working. It speeds up my day," Michael said, but he knew it was a lie. He despised large gatherings, since he loathed crowds and noise. He regarded himself as an introvert.

"Too much work and not enough fun makes Michael a dull boy," Raul snidely observed.

"All right, all right. Just don't bother me anymore. You'd best buy me a beer, because I'll only be there for an hour or two." Michael shot back.

Raul did not dispute this, and his eyes twinkled with delight. He finally persuaded his cousin to drop his customary reticence and appear on the social scene.

"With your gorgeous features and my charms, there's a one hundred percent chance we'll strike gold tonight."

Raul walked directly to the bar and bought two drinks when the cousins arrived at the club. He handed one to Michael, before excusing himself to visit the restroom. Two blonde chicks approached Michael while he was drinking his beer, and murmured softly in his ear.

"We came over to compliment you on your good looks. Do you have any plans for tomorrow? We'll be kayaking. Would you like to come along with us?"

"Me? That's too bad," Michael said. "I have plans for tomorrow, but it was wonderful to chat with you today. Have fun kayaking," Michael remarked as he walked away.

Raul grabbed another beer when he noticed the two stunning blondes conversing with his cousin.

"Hey Michael, what did those lovely ladies want?"

Michael shrugged and informed his cousin that they were going kayaking the next day.

"Well?" asked Raul.

"Well, what?"

"Did they invite you?"

"They did, in fact. But I will not waste my time on things that don't interest me. I have more important things to do than kayak."

"Michael, my God. Those women were attempting to seduce you. What's the matter with you?"

"I'm not interested at all."

Raul shook his head, dissatisfied with his cousin's demeanor. He then turned to face the ladies.

"Wait a minute! Are you looking for someone to join you tomorrow on a kayaking trip? I'm readily available."

The girls laughed, and Raul wrapped his arms around their shoulders while they chatted. Before they went outside, he winked at Michael.

It wasn't long before Michael was chatting to two lovely women. Even though he knew they were drawn to him, he never made advances or flirted with them. He was the epitome of a gentleman.

"What did you talk about with those girls?" Raul asked.

"Are you back again, Raul? Didn't you say you were going kayaking with those two gorgeous chicks tomorrow?" Michael asked, his lips pointing at the ladies.

"Hey, it's still early in the evening."

"I swear to God. You'll get it one of these days if you're not careful. Yes, we chatted a little. Those ladies did all the talking. I only listened. They told me they were on vacation here and provided me with their phone numbers if I wanted to come over tomorrow night. There's another party they're going to."

"Are we going?" Raul asked.

"What exactly do you mean by "we"?"

"Well, partner, we usually go together, right?" Raul gave him a wink. "Come on, dude; I despise crashing parties. I'd want to be invited for a change."

Michael gave a shaky nod.

"You're pitiful. Anyway, I'm exhausted and heading home. I'll catch up with you later."

"It's too early, Michael. There are still many lovely ladies to meet. What's the matter with you?"

"Call me an old-fashioned guy, but I like to let my actions speak for themselves. Before I contemplate getting closer to a lady, I want to get to know her first. I like to pursue rather than be pursued. And, as wonderful as this may appear, it makes me anxious when a lady I don't know flirts with me. This isn't normal!"

For a moment, Raul considered what his cousin had said.

"All right, more for me to serenade." Raul said as he bid farewell to his cousin.

On his way back home, Michael marched down the beach. He considered staying longer at the club, but he was wary about pushing things too far. It was one thing to see young girls freak out over a good-looking guy like him, but it was another to see older women do the same. He'd never been self-conscious about his appearance. Women liked to gaze at him and prod him in unusual ways and settings, but it did not entice him. Something in the back of his mind and heart told him there was a particular girl waiting for him.

As time passed, Michael built his company as the premier supplier of fresh seafood to upscale restaurants and fish markets around Honolulu, which led to his visit there. He even expanded his business by bringing fresh fish from the boat to their table. For a smooth delivery, Michael hired two people on Towi Island to pack them in boxes. Michael created a reputation for himself when he hooked and sold a 500-pound Pacific Bluefin tuna for a nice profit. He used the money to purchase a larger boat. Michael also bought a brand-new, top-of-the-line pickup truck and had it sent to Towi Island for his personal usage. For commercials, he continued to drive his father's old pickup truck.

.. ⚘ ..

MICHAEL HAD A HARD and exhausting morning delivering the last crate of fresh, live blue crabs to the Honolulu fish market. He immediately hurried to his boat and flung himself onto his bed. He was on his pillow, but his eyes wouldn't close. Fatigue took him quickly, and before he realized it, he was fast asleep. His stomach grumbled as he awakened. It was midday before he knew what time it was. Michael moved up to the little refrigerator, which only had empty ice cube trays in the top drawer. He examined the remaining shelves, which had ketchup, mustard, a bottle of water, and a few pieces of hard candy. Michael suckled on the hard candy. His stomach grumbled once more. He walked to a nearby deli, wearing shorts and slippers, to get something to eat. He reasoned that a nice cold beer to accompany his meal would be perfect.

As he stepped off the curb, he was about to encounter the meanest person ever walked the earth... and his destiny.

CHAPTER FIVE

"I'm old enough to go on vacation with my friends," Vanessa stated, as they heard her arguing with her parents early in the morning. It was her twenty-first birthday, and she planned to celebrate it in Hawaii with her SBP friends. Nothing changed. Vanessa was still behaving like a spoiled diva.

"I'm not sure what's making you so upset. We haven't said no yet, Vanessa," her mother remarked.

"Well, I just want to make sure you know what I want," Vanessa remarked, with the prettiest little pout.

"We know," her parents said in unison.

"Don't worry, Ness. We need to be in London on a business trip. It's too bad the Grandeville Resort in Waikiki is still under construction, but I'll have my secretary arrange your travel plans for you and your friends. Just promise me you'll be careful," her father said. "Agree?"

Vanessa nodded. "I agree! Thank you, Dad," Vanessa murmured, kissing and hugging him. Her father spoiled her rotten, and Vanessa knew well that she had taken advantage of him. Tom recognized it, but he did nothing to stop it. He wants his little princess to be happy.

• • ❧ • •

VANESSA AND HER COMPANIONS boarded Islander Airlines from Los Angeles to Honolulu, where warm and

cheerful flight attendants greeted them dressed in bright, traditional island attire. The soothing Hawaiian music comforted
the friends playing over the PA during boarding, and they were
fed delicious meals with authentic island flavors. Vanessa chose
a tropical drink while her girlfriends drank champagne.

The landing was perfect, and they even arrived early. The
girls waited for their bags to emerge from the baggage carousel.
Vanessa noticed a young, attractive man holding an orange
card with her name written in large, bold letters on it. Enrique,
their limousine driver, was pleasant and helpful. He took their
luggage and placed it in the trunk. Then he reached down to
pick up their carry-on luggage, but Vanessa refused to move.

"Do you need help with your bags, ma'am?" he asked.

"No!" she yelled. "I'd rather you didn't."

"I'm sorry," he responded with a smirk.

Vanessa saw it and gave Enrique a harsh look.

"Let me give you some advice. You never know who you'll
be dealing with, so be careful what you say or do. I want nothing to ruin my day, so I'll let this go, but if you keep doing this,
you won't have a job tomorrow. Comprende?" Vanessa stated.

"I'm sorry!" said Enrique.

Wow! What a bitch! he murmured to himself.

Vanessa instructed Enrique to drive them around the island, before dropping them off at their hotel in Waikiki. Enrique agreed, although it was a bittersweet experience. He
knew well that Vanessa's father had considerable power. Enrique had no choice, but worked hard to be the ideal tour
guide. He took them to places including Pearl Harbor, the
Bishop Museum, the Honolulu Museum of Art, Iolani Palace,
Ala Moana Beach Park, and Waikiki Beach. When the girls

became exhausted, Enrique drove them to Paradise Tower to check in.

Vanessa rented a black Aston Martin DB9 carbon edition convertible for their vacation. She and her friends took it for a spin down Ala Moana Boulevard, soaking in the sun. Vanessa acted with arrogance and malice, cutting off traffic and refusing to yield to crossing pedestrians as if she owned the road. She believed that since she was affluent, she had the authority to act and behave as she liked.

Meanwhile, Michael crossed the street to the MDLM Store to have some lunch. He was a few feet away from the curve when he heard a loud shriek. A vehicle was speeding and almost hit him. He looked up furiously, but something caught his eye—the most beautiful angel he had ever seen.

Vanessa jumped out of the car, cursing and criticizing Michael for walking too slowly on a busy roadway. She sped away, leaving the scent of burnt rubber on her tires, while Michael stunned in the corner, scratching his head and staring at the vehicle as it drove away.

$$\cdot \cdot \infty \cdot \cdot$$

VANESSA LOOKED AMAZING as she strolled to the beach with her bikini-clad girlfriends, wearing a little bikini, sunglasses, and a relaxing straw hat while sunbathing and flaunting her enviable curves. She grinned as she watched the attractive guys catch waves and ride them across the water. One surfer looked over and waving to her. Vanessa was having a good time, so she waved back and tossed a kiss in the air. It caught the surfer off guard and threw him off his surfboard, causing him to crash into the water. He attempted to jump back up, but the waves pushed him off the surfboard before he could even get on.

Vanessa and her pals laughed.

"Look what you did to that poor guy," Jennifer exclaimed.

Vanessa laughed so hard that everyone turned to look at her. The surfer noticed it and was humiliated, since the wave was pounding him. He rode the wave, but this time his surfboard toppled over.

"Whoa, that was a smooth ride," Samantha said.

The surfer could hear Vanessa and her pals howling with laughter. Embarrassed, the surfer bowed his head, and his shoulders sagged. His face flushed with shame, and he gave up and left.

The girls strolled along the shore, where they spotted thirty canoes of all shapes and sizes lined up together. They had missed the event for the day, which was a mixed crew of six in racing canoes. A single-boat race was scheduled for the next day.

The weather was bright, and the breeze was ideal for a leisurely ride. After looking at the yachts, Vanessa got the brilliant idea of renting a boat and taking them sailing.

"Hey, that'll be fun. I haven't sailed in a long time," Stephanie said, and everyone agreed.

"Great! Then it's settled," Vanessa answered, beaming.

She advised her friends to book a private cruise or charter a boat for an exhilarating afternoon sail. She said she'd meet them on the beach. Her friends nodded as they walked toward the waterfront.

Meanwhile, Michael had finished his lunch and enjoyed his beer while cleaning and testing the engine, preparing his boat to return home early the next day. Vanessa strolled along the beach, running her fingers into the white sand and burying her feet. She collected seashells, something she had done as a child. Vanessa was having a great time, since she had never seen so many shells in one location before. She had walked quite a way when she noticed a boat nearby—the only one on the dock. Vanessa hopped over the railing and climbed aboard, believing it was the boat her friends had rented. She went downstairs and glanced around. It was tiny, with a combined living and dining area with a TV and a dining table, as well as a small kitchen with a hot plate and a gas refrigerator. There was a bedroom with a full-size bed and a bathroom with a shower. She returned to the deck to look for her friends. She wondered where they were.

Michael had just finished checking the engine. He was unwinding on the deck of his boat, listening to the harsh sound of birds flying above the ocean and the soothing lapping of the waves against the hull. He was surprised when Vanessa ordered him to start the engine.

"Wait a minute. Am I on TV right now?" he asked, smiling. Michael watched reruns in the afternoon and thought he was being punked on some TV show by fooling people with unexpected situations. He looked around, but he saw no cameras or anyone.

"Start the engine," Vanessa said.

Michael scowled and rubbed his chin. "Excuse me, miss. Who are you and what are you doing in my boat? You made a mistake."

"The mistake is that you're standing there pretending you didn't hear me. Come on. Get this boat ready. We want to go sailing right now!"

Michael blinked, perplexed. "I own this boat, and it is not for hire."

When Michael explained she boarded the wrong boat, Vanessa brushed him off and just covered her ears. She was acting childish. Michael frowned and studied her. Then he froze. He recognized she was the same girl who had almost hit him on the street earlier. Michael thought she was cute as she pouted her lips. In fact, she was the most beautiful woman he had ever seen in his life.

Michael thought to himself, "She's a goddess." He'd never expected to see her again, and he took a moment to compose himself, a goofy grin pasted on his face. Michael didn't know why, but there was something about her that made him smile. He was taken with her. He had a strong desire for her.

"Whoever you are, dear princess, your request is my command," he said, bowing and curtsying. He played along by starting the boat motor to warm it up. Then he cleaned and straightened up the cabin. He pulled out the food he had purchased for his trip home and placed it on the dish. Michael even opened a pricey bottle of Dom Perignon that he had been saving for a special occasion. He put up a little table on the deck and put the plate with food and champagne on it. He had no idea why he was doing all that for that crazy woman.

"Would you like some cheese and crackers?" he asked. Michael was enjoying her company.

Vanessa accepted it without hesitation.

Michael poured a glass of champagne for Vanessa. He watched as she drank it all down in one gulp.

"Hmm, Dom Perignon, eh? I have to hand it to you. You have class."

Vanessa poured herself a hefty dosage of the beverage, flung it down, then poured another. She then ate more cheese and crackers without inviting Michael to join her.

"Why don't you take my picture? It'll stay longer."

Michael did not realize she was gazing at her, and was taken aback by the girl's candor.

"Oh, I'm sorry," Michael murmured as he walked away, scratching his head.

Vanessa poured herself another glass of champagne, flung it down, and then poured another. She fell asleep, intoxicated on the chair, and when Michael checked on her later, he didn't have the heart to wake her up while she was sleeping.

· · ᴏᴌᴏ · ·

VANESSA OPENED HER eyes to see that the sun had gone down, and the air had become considerably cooler. When she awoke, she clutched a lovely cushion and a blanket. She looked around, but didn't see any of her friends. Vanessa rose up, looked around, and saw her pals walking on the beach a few yards away. She motioned them over with her straw hat.

"What the heck are you doing here, Vanessa?" Rachel asked as she and her friends boarded the boat. "I don't know how many times we passed this boat, but we never thought you were in it. We were about to call the cops."

"What do you mean, you're looking for me? Isn't this the boat you rented?"

"No. We got to the marina, but the rental shop was out of boats. We even asked private boat owners whether they would consider renting out their vessels to us for a few hours, but no one seemed interested. Stephanie finally called Enrique's number. His uncle has a yacht, and he agreed to take us sailing. He'll meet us at the hotel early tomorrow morning."

"Then whose boat is this?" Vanessa asked.

That's when Michael spoke out.

"It's my boat. As I told you previously, it's not for hire."

"What? You let me eat and sleep here?" she yelled.

"Yes, because you didn't want to leave. I brought you food, and you even drank the entire bottle of Dom Perignon."

"Well, I never—"

Instead of appreciating Michael for his hospitality, Vanessa yelled at him, accusing him of taking advantage of her.

"You purposely kept me here. You knew I'd made a mistake, yet you still gave me food and champagne. And you intended to make me intoxicated so you could have your way with me!"

"I did not do such a thing, Miss. I told you multiple times that you made a mistake, but you didn't listen. You didn't want to leave."

Vanessa walked out, enraged. Her companions followed her and left Michael alone, still surprised by what had transpired, but not furious. It relieved him to see his "angel" again. He tried to deny it, but he knew he felt something for her.

Vanessa's friends smiled as they walked back to their car.

"You know, Vanessa," Samantha said, folding her arms across her chest. "He's a hottie!"

"He certainly is," Rachel concurred. "He could take me sailing any day." She then burst out laughing like a schoolgirl.

Vanessa stopped walking. She had a wide grin on her face.

"Yes, he is attractive, isn't he?"

"He reminds me of George Clooney, except he's younger!" Stephanie stated.

"No, that's not it. He appears familiar, as if he's someone I've recently met."

"Familiar? How so?" Rachel asked.

"I can't put my finger on it, but I feel... I don't know. That I've met him before."

Rachel joked, "Or maybe he reminds you of Chris Hemsworth or a younger Tom Cruise."

Vanessa had a feeling that wasn't the case. Michael wasn't her normal type, so what drew her to him? She brushed it aside, keeping her admiration buried deep inside and concealed from everyone.

· · ⌘ · ·

DANIEL, A HIGH SCHOOL buddy, called Michael. He was a server at Ernesto's, a well-known club inside Paradise Tower. Daniel knew Michael was in town and asked if he could assist him for two hours. Three of their employees called in sick, leaving them shorthanded. It was a hectic day for them because of the canoe race that weekend. The club was completely packed, yet there was still a huge line.

"Please, Michael, even if it's only for an hour or two. I urgently need help. My supervisor is yelling at me, and the customers are yelling at me. I'm losing my mind. Please come as soon as possible before I yell at myself."

Michael intended to relax and get a good night's sleep before sailing back home the next day, but he couldn't say no to his friend. Daniel was like a brother to him. He hurriedly show-ered and dressed. He was on his way in a flash.

Ernesto's was about a five-minute walk from the dock. Michael went into the kitchen from the back room. He noticed Daniel was moving far too fast as he put the dishes away. He knew his friend was tired.

There was no greeting: no hi or hello. As soon as Daniel saw him, he handed Michael a red apron, and Michael got to work cleaning tables. Daniel wasn't joking. Ernesto's was so crowded that they couldn't move. There was a long line outside waiting to get in, and Michael wondered how the club could accommodate them. Michael spent most of his time cleaning, stacking, washing, and arranging dishes. He did an outstand-ing job, which satisfied the owner, and asked if Michael could work for the weekend.

"We have more guests arriving, and we need all the help we can get. I'll compensate you for your time and trouble," said Ernesto, the owner and manager.

Michael thanked the man, but refused the offer, explaining that he wanted to go home early the next day. To the owner's delight, Michael remarked, "But I'll stay for a while to help."

"Thank you, Michael. That makes me happy. Remember, if you need a job, my door is always open for you," Ernesto joked.

Meanwhile, Vanessa and her friends returned to the hotel after cruising the boulevard. As they walked to the elevator to rest, they heard music and noticed a line to Ernesto's Club that went all the way to the lobby. It piqued Vanessa's interest, and she and her friends decided to check it out. Vanessa ges-tured for the hotel manager to come over, and then inquired what was all the commotion about, pointing her face toward the people lined up. According to the manager, Ernesto's was the city's trendiest nightclub.

"Once the sun goes down, the celebration starts and lasts all night at Ernesto's," the manager stated.

Vanessa nodded and urged him to arrange for them to have a VIP table, which the manager did.

Vanessa and her companions didn't waste time getting dressed. Everyone in the hotel lobby looked at the girls as they waited for the hotel manager. They were dressed in a black strapless party dress, black silk stockings, and black high heels. Even the hotel manager, who came seconds afterwards, continued shaking his head in admiration as he greeted them with adoration from head to toe. They resembled high-fashion supermodels.

The hotel manager led the girls in the VIP line to their table. They passed others who had been waiting in line for a long time to get inside the club, and raised their eyebrows in surprise. But the girls merely rolled their eyes and laughed at everyone.

"Wow!" Samantha exclaimed as she stepped into the club. "I love this place."

Vanessa looked around the enormous club. A sophisticated mahogany bar, modern artwork on the walls, and an open-air atrium with tiki torches and potted palms were among the features. The crowd became louder as they danced to classics from the 1970s and 1980s.

Because the ladies' table wasn't ready yet, the manager invited Vanessa and her pals to wait at the bar while they prepped their VIP table. Vanessa's head was racing with rage, but she didn't want to ruin her night. She held back a dramatic outburst and shrugged her shoulders, nodding her head as she and her pals walked into the bar.

"This will be an amazing vacation, I can tell," Rachel stated.

"Yes, I see that," Jennifer responded, looking at the attractive men who gave her the goo-goo eyes. "I love Hawaii. There are so many attractive males here, and only one tiny old me."

"Yeah, yeah. Those men aren't staring at you, Jen. Do you see that guy over by the water fountain? He's been staring at me ever since we arrived. Isn't he stunning?" Stephanie queried.

"That guy by the water fountain, you said? Let me check him out for you," Jennifer replied as she moved away suddenly. She returned a few minutes later, dejected.

"Well?" Stephanie inquired, her face tense.

"He was good looking all right, but he talked about himself endlessly. He's a complete bore. That guy is not your type, believe me."

"Oh, what a shame," Stephanie said, pouting her lips.

Vanessa let out a frustrated groan.

"I came here to have girl time, not only to flirt with boys. I don't have time for that right now. Let's have fun with just the six of us, OK?"

"I'm sorry, Vanessa. You're right. It's your birthday," Alexandra said. "All right, let's do this. It's a girls' night out! Let's get this party started."

As they shout, the girls high-five one another. They made a toast while sipping vodka. The Village People's *YMCA* rocked the dance floor. They danced, but it was difficult, as they kept bumping into others or treading on their toes. The lights were gloomy, the music was loud, and it was impossible to talk. It was extremely crowded and stuffy, so the girls took a break and returned to the bar.

"Hey," Stephanie remarked, out of the blue. "I've got an idea. We're in Hawaii to have a good time. How about we pick a secluded beach tomorrow so we can have it all to ourselves?"

"That is a fantastic concept. When Enrique picks us up tomorrow morning, we'll tell his uncle to take us cruising around the island, looking for that perfect beach for us," Rachel explained.

"Hmm... I have to hand it to you, ladies. That's the best idea I've heard today," Vanessa added.

Meanwhile, Michael was about to leave when Ernesto stopped him. He asked if he could stay for a few minutes longer to clean one last table. He may go after it.

"Don't worry, manager; I've got your back," Michael said.

· · ∾ · ·

VANESSA WAS GROWING impatient. They had been waiting much too long for their table. She signaled for her pals to follow her in an intense rage.

"Clean or not, we're sitting."

Meanwhile, Michael had just finished wiping the last table. He placed the dirty glasses and bottles on the tray. When he turned around, he didn't see Vanessa and accidentally hit her with the tray. The glasses flew everywhere. Vanessa was completely drenched. She was outraged.

"You foolish, stupid moron!" she yelled at the top of her lungs as she tried to wipe her dress. Her blood was boiling with rage, but as she looked up, she recognized Michael.

"You?"

Vanessa was thrilled to see him. She didn't know why, but she had longed to see him again, and there he was, standing in front of her. Vanessa wanted to apologize for their earlier encounter, but she felt uneasy because all eyes were on them. She couldn't let her friends see her talking to an ordinary bus-boy, and she let her pride get in the way. Without warning, she grabbed a glass of wine from the adjacent table and threw it at Michael.

For the next few moments, the music stopped. People stopped dancing. The lights came on, and Michael was drenched. His face flushed with shame.

Ernesto witnessed what had occurred and came to Michael's rescue. He patted him on the back and urged him to go home. Michael went away without looking back. Vanessa let her pride get the best of her again. She stormed out, screamed, and pursued Michael as he went out.

"You will never work in this town again, you fool!" she said. Her rage seemed to escalate.

Michael turned around and recognized Vanessa. Oh, how he wished to see her again. It was a remarkable coincidence to meet her under different circumstances, a bizarre twist of fate. It was incredible.

"Did you hear me, peasant?"

Michael was jolted back to reality. He was enraged by what she had called him. He gnashed his teeth and said, "My name is Michael, not a moron and certainly not a peasant!"

Without expecting it, Michael planted a lusty kiss on her lips, which lasted until Vanessa pulled him away. All eyes were on them. Michael walked away without looking at anyone, leaving Vanessa and her friends dumbfounded.

Vanessa touched her lips with her fingertips, still sensing him there. She'd never forget that beautiful, stolen kiss.

CHAPTER SIX

E nrique was furious. He'd been pacing in the hotel lobby for two hours, waiting. He checked his watch for the tenth time. It was nine o'clock. He expected the girls to be ready by seven a.m. Enrique was irritated because he had waited much too long. He took a scrap of paper, scribbled a note on it, and handed it to the hotel clerk. He stormed out of the building, yelling and swearing.

The girls partied into the early hours of the morning at Ernesto's, dancing on top of tables and screaming to the music. The ladies lived their lives to the fullest, without a worry in the world. They stayed until closing time and were so intoxicated that the hotel staff had to take them back to their room. Except for Jennifer, who had just finished taking a shower, everyone else was in discomfort from the night before and had difficulty standing. Suddenly, there was a knock on the door. Jennifer opened it to see the bellboy holding a silver platter with a note on it. He'd been standing at the door for a while, since no one had answered his knock. Jennifer gasped as he handed her the note. She gave him a nod, and the bellboy saluted and went off to the elevators.

Jennifer scowled as she read the message. She dialed Enrique's number and was happy he answered the phone, but his anger was still clear in his voice. Jennifer did not apologize, but offered to pay more for the inconvenience and rescheduled the boat to be ready early the next morning, which Enrique accepted. Never mind that he was unhappy earlier; he was getting a big commission from his uncle, since the girls had chartered the yacht for the weekend. He was certain he would receive significant tips for his services, and he planned to use the money to put down on a new car.

.. ᑎᏉᏂ ..

"WE DECLARE THIS TO be your special day. You're going with us because your birthday surprise is waiting for you," the girls informed Vanessa as she awoke.

Vanessa enjoyed surprises and was excited to find out what her friends had prepared for her birthday. The girls treated her to a luxury spa experience, a pampering day of relaxation that included a facial, body treatment, manicure, and pedicure. Their next visit was an incredible shopping spree, splurging on pricey dresses, purses, and perfumes. The last stop was back at their hotel, where the girls took Vanessa down a long corridor that led to an atrium filled with flowers, trees, and a breathtaking waterfall. The staff greeted them with a friendly "aloha," decked them with fresh leis, and offered them a Mai Tai. Vanessa was blown away.

"What did you guys do? This place is amazing," she added, beaming.

"Just wait and see," her friends said.

Vanessa's grins faded to frowns as they reached the venue's entrance, and her excitement quickly turned to anger when she realized where they were heading. She detested luaus. She thought they were tacky. Even though the staff were pleasant and they served exquisite, authentic Hawaiian food, and the servers kept their drinks flowing, she despised them. While her friends enjoyed the show, Vanessa made it clear to them that she hated it. She didn't touch her food and kept sipping her beverages only.

"Ness, are you all right? Don't tell me you don't like your birthday present?"

Before Vanessa could respond, the server had put the roasted pig's head on the table as an adornment. She stepped back, her eyes wide and horrified.

"Do you mind? Get this awful thing out of my face."

The server was shaken and embarrassed after being surprised by Vanessa's abrupt outburst. He was so scared that his fingers clenched on the tray as he scooped up the pig's head from the table to keep it from dropping to the floor. He struggled to take a breath.

Vanessa, who was terrified of luaus, was eight years old when her parents took her to an authentic luau in Hawaii. She sat in the front row, on cushions, so she could watch and enjoy the show. Vanessa loved the fire dance and hula dancing. The spread was diverse and extensive. Sweet lobster cooked to perfection, braised short ribs, and grilled chicken were among the dishes. Salads, poi, and sweets such as coconut pudding, mango tarts, chocolate, and other pastries were available. Vanessa was at the buffet table checking out the rest of the food when she shrieked in terror at the sight of the whole roasted pig with an apple in its mouth. It terrified her half to death, but the worst thing was seeing everyone laugh at her. She wished she could curl up in a miserable cave. From then on, she despised luaus.

"How could I be calm after this debacle? It was a nightmare! It did not sit well with me. Since my parents paid for my trip and it's my birthday, I will choose where, when, and what to do from now on. I appreciate the thought, but no thanks," Vanessa told her friends.

"We were simply trying to make you happy on your birthday. We thought you loved luaus. I'm sorry," Rachel said.

Vanessa's sarcasm proved to be baseless when she realized how concerned her friends were about her.

"Okay, I forgive you!" she murmured this as they hugged.

"Yes! It's time to go sailing!" said the girls.

Vanessa phoned the hotel manager when they returned to their room. She ordered imported caviar, cheese, and crackers, a dozen bottles of the most expensive wine and champagne, fruits, and an unending salad bar for their boat cruise the next day. She also instructed the manager to purchase three of the largest and most sturdy iceboxes money could buy to keep the food fresh for days.

"I want our weekend getaway to be first class all the way. Three lovely days of amazing inter-island cruising," she remarked.

Vanessa turned on the music, and Gloria Estefan's "Conga" played. The girls lip-synced the song, formed a conga line, and danced around the room.

• • ❧ • •

ENRIQUE ARRIVED AT the hotel early the next morning to pick up the girls. He reasoned that if they didn't show up again, he would charge them for his time. To his amazement and delight, the girls were waiting for him in the lobby, dressed warmly. Vanessa wore a basic white halter top with pleated denim shorts and a pink sweater. Jennifer and Samantha chose Bermuda shorts and a white tee. Stephanie wore blue floral shorts and a matching top, while Rachel and Alexandra wore blue sundresses. They couldn't wait to start their cruise, so they dashed to the marina.

Stephanie, Rachel, Samantha, Alexandra, Vanessa, Jennifer, Enrique, and Marco, the boat's skipper, were among the eight people on board.

The girls' partying became louder from the start of the trip, as they drank all day and all night. The second day began early in the morning. Enrique prepared an excellent espresso mocha using Hawaiian Kona coffee, which the girls enjoyed. Jennifer suggested they swim before continuing on the cruise. Marco turned off the motor, and everyone leaped from the boat into the ocean for a relaxing dip in the clear blue sea. Vanessa was tired and content to sunbathe on the deck in her little bikini.

After a while, everyone returned to the boat, and the girls joined Vanessa in sunbathing on the deck, while Stephanie continued to strike herself and even fell from her chair as bugs attacked her. Marco started the engine. They resumed their journey while the rain fell. Marco was unconcerned. It was only a little drizzle.

Enrique turned out to be a fantastic cook. He expected them to be back in Honolulu by two o'clock in the afternoon the next day, so he treated the girls to a special dinner on their last night. He wanted to impress them with his culinary abilities. Enrique laid out the food on the table. Except for the Kalua pig, the menu included classic luau cuisine. The girls dressed up and were ready to party again. They were excited to try Enrique's creations, but as soon as Vanessa saw the food, she threw up.

"What's wrong?" Enrique asked.

"I despise Hawaiian food."

"I'm sorry. I didn't know," Enrique said.

"Don't worry, Enrique. She'll get over it," Stephanie said.

"Don't mind me. I'll sit here and enjoy this lovely drink," Vanessa stated as she opened a bottle of champagne.

Enrique handed Vanessa a platter of spinach salad, and she nibbled on it. She then drank even more champagne. Meanwhile, her friends ate and praised Enrique for the delicious meal.

"Perhaps we should keep you as our cook while we're here."

"Anytime," Enrique laughed.

"Come on, guys, let's dance," Vanessa muttered, her words slurred.

"Are you getting tipsy already?" Rachel asked, her tone filled with skepticism.

Vanessa pursed her lips. "Just a bit," she responded, without slurring as much this time.

"Did you eat anything?"

"Yes, I had that green thing on my plate."

"Do you mean the spinach salad?"

"Yeah, green salad."

Rachel took the bottle away from Vanessa.

"Hey, give that back!"

"It's no surprise you're drunk." Rachel held up the empty bottle.

"Come on, girls. It's my birthday. Let's drink and have fun," Vanessa said.

The cork flew from the champagne bottle across the room with a sound as loud as a gunshot. Everyone drank, and then they poured another. Laughter rang out as they poured another one. This went on through the night until there was only one bottle of champagne left on the table. After a night of heavy drinking, the girls passed out. Vanessa ate very little during the day, so drinking champagne all night had a greater impact on her.

Meanwhile, after looking out to sea, Marco saw the sky was dismal. He always checked the weather report before sailing, and it was unexpected and not in the forecast. Marco constantly prioritized safety and would never jeopardize his own or his passengers' lives. He was an experienced sailor who understood how to handle the situation efficiently. Marco knew not to panic, as everyone depended on him, but he also knew it could be something serious. Unfortunately, he had little time to think. They were caught in a violent storm, and the boat was crashing into the wind. The captain radioed for help and gave their coordinates, but the signal was weak. With the loss of visibility, high seas posed a hazard. When the ship soon filled up with water, Marco retrieved his emergency supplies bag, which included a first-aid kit, a flashlight, and a blanket, and slung it on his back. Marco alerted Enrique and told him to protect the girls. Enrique had to shake the girls and cry out to them many times before they woke up. He handed each of them a life jacket, and the girls knew what it meant. They panicked.

Vanessa was still unconscious. Enrique smacked her a few times, but she was too drunk to wake up. Enrique slipped the life jacket on her and fastened it around her waist. He tied her from a metal table so she wouldn't fall, and intended to return to her after he checked on the other girls.

The storm resumed its attack on the boat. There was no use in attempting to fight the wind, as it became increasingly powerful. Marco came to a halt and kept his position, which seemed to work as he maintained control of the vessel. He kept sailing without incident until a big gust hit them and the powerful currents pushed them off course. It caused them to evacuate the ship, and they jumped out one by one until the boat catapulted out of the water and flipped on its side. Thankfully, Marco inflated the life raft before the boat sank. Vanessa's friends hung on to three enormous iceboxes that floated in the sea. They climbed on top, but there was no way they could help Vanessa. They couldn't reach her because she was drifting away.

The cool water awakened Vanessa. She opened her eyes to find herself submerged. Vanessa attempted to steer herself back into the open air, but it was really difficult. She clung to the metal table, floating in a catatonic condition as the waves took her away. Vanessa's friends watched in horror and could do nothing but cry as she drifted away and eventually vanished. The girls were distraught by the loss of their dearest friend.

Marco, Enrique, and the girls found themselves adrift and alone on the high seas. They survived by sipping the wine and food from the iceboxes, eating and drinking a little at a time. Marco connected the iceboxes and the life raft with the blanket he tore up to keep them together. The girls commended Vanessa for purchasing pricey, top-of-the-line, waterproof, and durable iceboxes that did not capsize in the inclement weather. They drifted for many days until the Coast Guard located them and brought an end to their nightmare.

Following their rescue, the hospital staff treated them for acute dehydration, malnutrition, and severe sunburn. They were heartbroken about the demise of their friend, Vanessa, but grateful to be alive. After they had healed, the doctors released them to their family.

The successful rescue mission made headlines around the world.

"SOCIALITE VANESSA FLORENCE GRANDEVILLE IS STILL MISSING," a newspaper headline read. Vanessa's family spokesperson stated, "We can affirm they have rescued five females and two males. We are still looking for Miss Vanessa Florence Grandeville. The family is coordinating with local authorities and the government to find her."

CHAPTER SEVEN

Vanessa opened her eyes, afloat on her improvised raft, as the sun beat down on her skin. She glanced around and was shocked to find herself at sea, with no land in sight. Vanessa initially assumed she was dreaming, but when she fell into the water, she knew she wasn't. She screamed and cried, but no one could hear her. Vanessa passed out quickly as the heavy downpour persisted. She drifted for many more days. She fell into the water and attempted to get back up, and the metal table tipped over many times. Vanessa climbed to the top again. She paddled as hard as possible, believing it would get her to safety, but her arms ached. It was a miracle she survived on the rainwater she had scooped up with her hands.

• • ⌘ • •

MICHAEL HAD RETURNED to Towi Island and was out at sea fishing. Several days had passed, but he was still fuming over what had happened to him at the club in Honolulu.

"What a disaster," he said. "It's not like me to lose my temper, but that woman was horrible. She was the worst creature I have ever met." He then paused for a moment to reflect. "However, why did I feel my heart was yearning for her? And that lengthy kiss I laid on her lips? What exactly was that? And why do I have the impression she's the one who got away?"

Michael knew that fishing after a good rain was the best time to catch fish. It was the period when they were more active as the oxygen level in the water increased. He flung the net high into the air, and it dropped into the water, creating hundreds of ripples. Then it sank to the bottom.

Michael brought the net back out of the water and onto the boat to see what he had caught. There were only anchovies, not worth a second glance. He cast his net again, but it came back empty. Michael went to a new location and started it again. He drifted through the water for what seemed like a lifetime, with little success. With a sigh and prayer, Michael moved a little further and tossed his fishing net one last time. To his amazement, when he dragged the net back out of the water, it was heavy, since he couldn't pull it. Michael believed he had caught the biggest fish of his life. This invigorated him, and he pulled more, but the stronger he pulled, the tighter it became. When he dragged the net in and examined the metal thing attached to it, his excitement quickly changed to confusion. His eyes widened in disbelief. There was a corpse knotted in the middle.

"Oh my God!" Michael freaked out. It was the first time he had seen a dead body.

It shifted unexpectedly. Michael got terrified and screamed. The body moved again, and it was breathing. Michael looked over the net and saw it was a woman. He lifted the net that was covering her face, and he received the shock of his life when he recognized who it was. Michael, perplexed, continued backing up and fell overboard.

Meanwhile, Vanessa had a dream in which she danced with the most attractive man in the room. He pulled her close as they rocked to the soothing music. It felt both tranquil and weird. Then she heard something passing overhead. She couldn't tell if she was asleep or awake. She strained to open her eyes and saw a hooded figure holding her. Her strength had worn out, and her thoughts had become jumbled. She couldn't tell the difference between a dream and reality. Vanessa could hear an engine running somewhere in the night. She gazed at the hooded guy again, and that was the last thing she saw before passing out.

Vanessa awoke after a lengthy period of unconsciousness. Everything was a misty gray. She winced when she shifted her head. She looked around the room. It was strange, a location she had never been to before. She felt dreadful, as though the room was spinning as she touched her head with a bandage. She attempted to stand, but became disoriented and passed out again.

· · ❧ · ·

"SHE'S COMING AROUND. Call the doctor right away!" said the nurse.

Vanessa could just make out a faint voice. She blinked her eyes awake and concentrated on her surroundings. She noticed a bald man wearing a lab coat and a stethoscope around his neck, smiling at her. A nurse took her blood pressure. She strained to sit up, but her head ached. She touched it and felt the huge bandage on her head again.

"Where am I?" a perplexed Vanessa inquired.

"My name is Dr. Fletcher. You are here at Towi Medical Center. You've been here for nearly a week. We were afraid you wouldn't wake up."

"A week?" Vanessa wondered, struggling to get out of bed.

"Just lie down. You're not going anywhere with a big bump on your head," the doctor said as he put her back on the bed. "Do you remember what happened to you?"

Vanessa frowned. She couldn't recall anything, no matter how hard she tried. Her memories were erased. It was incomprehensible. Why couldn't she remember?

"What happened? What am I doing here?" she asked and yelled as loudly as she could while kicking her feet.

The doctor was ready to give Vanessa some medication to calm her down when a handsome man entered the room and tapped on his shoulder. He pulled up a chair and sat close to Vanessa's bed.

"Doc, I've got this. Don't worry," he said, smiling.

Dr. Fletcher nodded and motioned to the staff, and they all left the room. When they were alone, Michael turned to Vanessa.

"How are you feeling?" he asked.

Vanessa looked at this guy's gentle face with a tired, puzzled expression. She didn't recognize the man. She stirred once more.

"Who are you? What am I doing here?" she asked while looking at the man.

Michael scowled. Their paths only crossed a few times in one day, but he was certain she would remember him, especially the way she shouted and embarrassed him in front of people at Ernesto's. What about the time she yelled at him on his boat or nearly struck him with her car? And who could forget the kiss they shared?

"Seriously? You don't remember me?"

"Would I ask you if I knew?" Vanessa smirked.

Nothing has changed. Michael muttered to himself. *She is still the rudest person I know.*

Vanessa asked, "What did you say?"

"Nothing. My name is Michael. You're in the hospital."

"I know I'm in the hospital. The doctor was here, remember? He told me. What I need to know is what I'm doing here. What happened to me?" Vanessa asked, her head resting on her hand. "Ouch!"

"Do not move. Just rest," Michael said. "To answer your questions, I found you unconscious at sea. I went out on my boat fishing and thought I'd caught the largest fish ever. It turned out to be just you, so I brought you here to make sure you're OK. Are you OK?"

"I guess. I'm not sure."

"What is your name?" Michael asked, pretending he didn't know her, although he heard her friends call her Vanessa while they were on his boat. Michael purposefully avoided discussing what he knew about her. He intended to put her to the test. He did not know why.

"My name is..." she stopped. "For the love of God, I know what my name is. I mean, I should remember my name. This is ridiculous! For God's sake, what is my name?" Vanessa yelled in frustration.

"Do you know what happened to you? Why were you at sea?"

Vanessa sighed and then continued in a gentle, calm voice. "I'm sorry, Michael. I didn't intend to be harsh, but it's so irritating to not know who I am."

Michael couldn't believe it, and it left him stunned. The meanest person on the planet knew how to apologize, but what was this business that she had no memory of the events?

When Michael was about to leave the room to talk to Dr. Fletcher, he heard Vanessa call his name. She asked where he was going. Michael smiled and assured her she was in excellent hands at the hospital, and that the doctors and their staff would take good care of her.

Vanessa struggled to sit up, keeping her throbbing head as motionless as possible, but Michael pushed her back.

"Please, Michael, don't leave yet. Don't leave me here," she implored.

"Don't worry," he soothed her. "You're in excellent hands here. You are welcome to stay as long as you like. I'm sorry, but I have to leave. The weather is pleasant, and I must return to the water to catch fish. That's my job. I'm a fisherman!" Michael stated.

Vanessa burst into tears. She felt helpless. She didn't know anyone but Michael, whom she felt saved her life. Vanessa twisted her head again. Dr. Fletcher entered and gave Vanessa a light sedative to calm her down. She fell asleep just a few moments later.

Michael sat next to her, watching her sleep. He then asked Dr. Fletcher why Vanessa could remember nothing.

"I assume she has amnesia. We need to do further tests to be certain. In the meantime, she needs to stay here for a few days until we can release her. She can rest at home."

There was a moment of silence. Michael chuckled to himself, then nodded his head, but with a peculiar expression on his face.

Amnesia? he grumbled to himself as he rubbed his chin.

"Is there something you wish to tell me, Michael?" asked the doctor when he saw him acting suspiciously.

Michael scratched the back of his neck.

"How long does her amnesia last, Doc?"

"We don't know. It might be days, months, or years. The good news is Vanessa is no longer in danger."

"Doc, do me a favor and don't tell anyone I brought her here."

"But why Michael?"

Michael hesitated to respond, and the silence stretched deeper.

"Michael, I've known you since you were born. The least you could do is trust me and tell me the truth. What is going on? You've been checking up on her every day. Do you know who she is? What happened to her?"

Michael considered telling the doctor how he met Vanessa, but decided it wasn't the proper moment. He gazed at her frail body, and despite the circumstances, he was reluctant to leave her. He bit his lower lip, crossed his fingers behind his back, and told the first lie of his life.

"All right, Doc. I'll tell you. Her name is Vanessa, and she is my wife. We got married in Honolulu. We had an accident at sea, and she went overboard. I didn't want you to tell anyone about our wedding because it's complicated. Just trust me, Doc."

"Why didn't you say so in the first place? That is wonderful. I'm pleased to hear it, Michael. I didn't mean the accident; I meant getting married. It was time you settled down. I'm sorry about her amnesia. We will continue to monitor her situation.

We'll call you when she's ready to go home, but she'll need to come back here in a week for a check-up."

Michael nodded and thanked the doctor. He walked out of the hospital, dazed and confused.

What am I doing? Why am I interested in helping the woman who has made my life miserable since I met her? Now she'll be staying in my house, and I'll have to look after her. If she weren't so attractive, I might get over the awful experience I've had with her.

Michael sighed as he walked away. He did not go fishing. Michael went home and cleaned his house. He also went to the store and bought food and other items he believed Vanessa might need while living with him.

The next day, Michael paid her a visit again at the hospital. He found her sitting on the bed as the nurse took her blood pressure. Vanessa smiled at him.

Dr. Fletcher entered the room and looked through Vanessa's record.

"Everything appears normal. You seemed in good physical condition, except for a few bruises that will heal in a few days."

"How about my memory loss, doctor? How temporary is it?"

"I'm sorry to say we don't know. We will continue to monitor your progress. You must return in a week so that we can reassess your condition. In the meantime, we will release you soon. I won't be here. I'll be visiting my daughter and her husband in Japan. He is in the military. My daughter will give birth at any moment now. But I want you to come back, and Dr. Phillips will examine you."

Vanessa nodded. Dr. Fletcher excused himself as he took Michael's arm on his way out.

"We conducted a thorough examination. Vanessa had forgotten who she was, where she came from, and her entire life history. She had a horrific sea experience. Try not to let her think too much. In most situations, her memory will return within a few days or months. We don't know for sure. We will monitor her progress."

Michael nodded.

"How long will you stay in Japan, Doc?"

"I'm not sure, Michael. It depends on my daughter's condition. She wants me to stay longer this time. If you're worried, Dr. Phillips is here to help. Vanessa is in great hands."

"Thank you, Doc. Have a safe trip, and don't eat too much Japanese food, please. It's your favorite food. You'll gain too much weight," Michael teased.

Dr. Fletcher chuckled.

"You silly boy!"

·· ❧ ··

TWO DAYS HAD PASSED when Michael received a call from the hospital telling him that the doctor had discharged Vanessa.

"That's fantastic news. When shall I pick her up?" he inquired.

"Dr. Fletcher just signed the release form. You may come and get her right now," the nurse said.

"I'll be there. Thank you for calling."

Michael whistled and grinned as he dressed.

"It's payback time. It's payback time," he sings loudly to his made-up tune. A few moments later, he pulled out of the driveway and proceeded toward the hospital.

Meanwhile, Vanessa sat in her room, waiting for someone to arrive to take her home. By this time, she knew her name. The hospital staff had addressed her by her first name. She had seen Dr. Fletcher earlier in the day, and he gave her instructions to repeat the prescription medication if the pain persisted. Otherwise, if she had any problems, she had to call the hospital immediately.

A few minutes later, the nurse entered and handed her a card with her next appointment written on it. They gave Vanessa a copy of the release form, instructions, and medications to take. The nurse informed her that a family member was on his way up to pick her up.

Great! I have a family. Vanessa's lips twisted into a faint grin.

The nurse left, but returned a short while later, pushing a wheelchair.

"All right, Vanessa, here's your ride. Someone is on their way to pick you up right now."

Vanessa raised her eyebrows at the wheelchair.

"Really, I'm good. I don't need it."

"I'm sorry, Vanessa, but you must. It's the hospital's policies."

"Seriously, I don't—"

"Vanessa, don't argue. Just sit."

Vanessa turned around when she heard a familiar voice.

"Michael, what are you doing here?" she grinned.

"I'm here to pick you up."

Vanessa's heart raced in her chest at the sight of him. She became distressed suddenly. Michael may have been a relative—a cousin or a brother? She wasn't sure why, but the notion made her shudder. That thought did not sit well with her. Her mind was screaming "no," and her heart was pounding.

"Are you OK, Vanessa?" Michael asked when she didn't answer.

Vanessa shook her head at him. She sat in the wheelchair, and the nurse wheeled her outside and stood with her while Michael went to get his truck. He pulled up next to them, stepped out, and helped Vanessa get into the front seat.

Vanessa couldn't resist the urge to ask while driving home.

"Michael, who are you again, and how are we related?"

Michael drawled; his face expressionless.

"You don't remember me? I'm your husband."

CHAPTER EIGHT

Getting even is the sweetest retribution, Michael thought to himself as he shook his head with a grin and finessed his hair in the rear-view mirror of his vehicle. *I occasionally astound myself with brilliant ideas.*

Michael laughed again. But deep down, he knew it was a bad thing to do to anyone. His parents didn't raise him that way, but he believed Vanessa needed a lesson in proper etiquette.

To make his plan work, he drove Vanessa around Towi Island "to stimulate her memory," as he explained. He was happy with his clever idea. He took his left hand off the steering wheel and pointed to some of the most beautiful spots for swimming, fishing, and snorkeling.

Vanessa shook her head as she looked around. She couldn't recognize any of it. Vanessa gazed at Michael, a stranger to her, relieved to learn he wasn't a relative or sibling. It still puzzled her why Michael didn't answer any of her queries about what she was doing at sea, and why he kept asking her name at the hospital as if he didn't know her. Some of what he'd told her before didn't make sense.

Vanessa tried hard to remember, but she was disoriented and thought her amnesia had changed her life. She glanced at Michael again, unsure whether she could trust him, but he was the only one who had shown his loyalty. He was the only one she felt comfortable with. She resisted him for as long as she could, but there was something in the way he smiled, or perhaps it was his eyes. Something in those brilliant eyes...

Vanessa exhaled a sigh. She took a moment to accept that this was her life.

"How's your head?" Michael asked, interrupting her thoughts. He was attempting to break the tension between them.

"Still attached!" Vanessa responded.

Michael's demeanor shifted. "Excuse me?" he asked.

Vanessa gave a shaky nod.

"Oh, I'm sorry. I mean, I still remember nothing about myself, my life, you..." she sighed.

Michael pretended to be a loving husband. As he drove, he wrapped his arm around her and moved her to rest on his shoulder. Vanessa didn't mind and thought it felt good.

It was dark when they came to a dilapidated hovel. As Vanessa stepped out of the truck, her jaw dropped. Her first idea, after her horror had passed, was to find a lighter and burn the house down.

She whispered, mostly to herself, "This can't be real."

"Well, here it is! Our tiny dwelling. Home, sweet home!" Michael said, as he pushed her forward to the door.

Vanessa took a deep breath and swallowed hard. Amnesia or not, she could tell when something was amiss. Vanessa felt her heart pounding in her chest. She came to a halt, unable to take another step. Her legs were as hard as lead. She tried to run away, but her feet were stuck in the concrete.

She entered the ramshackle house, her heart sickening at the sight of the dreadful surroundings. It was a large room with a sink and a cupboard. There was just one little window, and she believed the sunlight only illuminated a small portion of the room. The floor was made of raw dirt. The only furniture was a cot in the corner and a tiny table with two chairs. There was no privacy. Vanessa felt her world shatter around her. She struggled to take a breath. She felt crammed and constrained. Vanessa sensed the ceiling collapsing and the walls closing in on her. She thought the house was too tiny to live in. How did she stay there? Worst of all, there was no bathroom, and she needed to use it. That was the turning point in her life. She couldn't handle it anymore.

"I don't live in a hovel!" she screamed.

"Vanessa, relax. The neighbors will hear you."

"I'm sorry, Michael, but I despise this place. How can anybody live in a house where the living room, bedroom, and kitchen are all in the same room?"

"I'm surprised you say that considering you love this place."

"Did I? I'm sorry, Michael. I'm not sure why I feel like I've never been to a place like this before."

"It must be your amnesia. It'll come to you, eventually. Don't worry. I can hang a curtain to separate the bedroom from the living and kitchen areas. I'll hang a giant mirror on the living room wall to make the space look larger than it is," he suggested.

Vanessa trembled at the notion. "Could you tell me where the bathroom is?"

"Go outside."

Vanessa shuddered again. She was afraid of that. The horrible vision made her heart skip a beat. She struggled to take a breath. She looked outside, and the outhouse was sitting in a

convenient open space in the backyard, and she had no intention of going there in the dark.

"Are you insane? I don't want to go there. There might be
rats and snakes."

Michael smiled when he saw Vanessa's hesitation. He asked
her to wait a second while he got a flashlight from the drawer.
They walked in the dark, and Vanessa entered after a brief
pause, while Michael waited outside. She flipped on the light
and took a glance around. It's not what she expected. She had
to admit it had a few features. It was a modern-day outhouse. It
was made of plywood and had flowing water. There was a mar-
ble countertop around the sink and a large white metal shower
stall. She felt happy. The outhouse was much better than their
house. She didn't mind living there at all.

When they returned to the house, Michael urged Vanessa
to rest while he went to get their food. Vanessa nodded as she
cuddled under the cover on the cot. She remained in that position until she fell asleep.

Vanessa awoke cold and hungry in the early hours of the
morning. She pondered where Michael could be. She pushed
herself back to her feet and wiped her eyes. There was no sign
of him anywhere. She looked around the house, scratching her
head. When she opened the little window, she realized they
lived in a small cottage behind a large house, surrounded by
flower beds, a vegetable garden, and fruit trees. Her stomach
grumbled. She looked to see whether Michael had left her any
food. There were none.

Her stomach grumbled again.

*Why did Michael leave me in this condition and without
food?*

Vanessa paced across the room. She knew she'd pass out soon if she didn't eat something. Vanessa went to the big house to see if anyone was there, but she didn't hear or see anyone. Then she noticed scrumptious fruit hanging from the branches. Vanessa picked one, wiped the dust off on her shirt, and bit into it, discovering that it was exactly what she needed for breakfast.

She returned to the cottage in search of something to drink, but there was nothing in the cabinet. Vanessa turned on the tap, but there was no water coming out. She returned to the big house to see if anyone was home. She knocked on the door and yelled out, "Hello?" but no one replied. Vanessa twisted the doorknob, and it opened. She entered gently, so that the floor would not creak.

"Hello? The door is open. Could I please have a glass of water?"

Only her voice could be heard in the spacious room. She waited, but no one responded. She saw the refrigerator, so she opened it, grabbed a bottle of water, and ran as fast as she could.

"Vanessa!"

Vanessa had barely walked past the fruit trees when she heard her name shouted. She came to a halt and looked around, but no one was in sight.

"Vanessa!"

Vanessa heard her name again and took a step back toward the house, terrified. She heard the door creak behind her. She slowly turned around to see Michael standing at the door with his arms folded across his chest.

Vanessa frowned, puzzled, staring at him.

"What are you doing here? Where have you been? Did you know I was freaking out looking for you?" asked Vanessa.

Michael laughed. "I was about to get you when I saw you sneak out with the bottle of water," he continued, smiling. It was more of a smirk-grimace smile, but it was a smile.

"I'm sorry, Michael. I know it's wrong, but I was hungry and thirsty. You didn't leave any food in the house. Why didn't you wake me up?"

"It's not important what happened. Come on in, let's eat breakfast!"

"What do you mean, come inside? Do you think the landlord is OK with it? Do you work here?"

"Not exactly. I mean, we live here."

"This is our house?"

"Uh-huh," he said.

"Why would you do that? Why would you let me believe we live in a run-down house?"

Michael took a deep breath before responding. It appeared as though he was praying and asking for forgiveness for what was to come.

Here comes another lie, he told himself.

"I'm sorry, Vanessa. We made memories in that wooden shed, and I thought it might help you remember."

Vanessa lifted her brows and gave him a dubious look.

"Are you certain that's the only reason?"

Michael couldn't look her in the eyes. He knew she'd see straight through him.

"All right, let's forget about it and have some breakfast," Michael remarked, as he wrapped his arm around her.

Vanessa relaxed a little, but she kept her gaze fixed on Michael as he led her to the dining room. Michael pulled out a chair for her to sit on, and she had to admit it impressed her that her "husband" was a gentleman. Then Michael went to work. Vanessa observed him cracking eggs, beating them until they foamed, then pouring them into the skillet.

"Bam!"

Michael was dancing like a fool, mimicking Emeril Lagasse. He stood at the stove, holding a spatula, and shuffled the eggs in the pan. Vanessa grinned quietly, amused by him.

She looked around the house and realized it was a castle compared to the wooden hut where she had stayed and slept the night before. It overjoyed her to discover there was indoor plumbing. She smiled at the prospect of not having to return to the place she thought was their home.

They lived on a two-acre property in a spacious three-bedroom, two-bath bungalow-style house. She was taken aback. Michael said he inherited it from his parents. In the living area, the furniture was clean, uncluttered, and simple. She learned that Michael's father had built the wooden shed for his woodworking. Vanessa smiled with approval, but Michael misinterpreted it as an insult.

"I know what you're thinking," he said. "Our house is very tiny compared to..." His voice became hushed. He almost said "enormous house" by accident. "I mean, this is the best I can do for you."

Vanessa's riches were obvious to Michael, because she flaunted them on his boat, at Ernesto's Club, and while driving the sports vehicle that nearly hit him.

"Let me give you a tour of the house. This is our bedroom," Michael stated as he pushed the door open further.

Vanessa followed him into a spacious, paneled room with high ceilings and peered around. The room had a king-size bed, an antique Victorian dresser with a wide mirror, matching nightstands, and crystal lamps on each side. Michael's mother had bought them, and he didn't have the heart to get rid of them. There were large his and her closets next to each other. Vanessa opened the first closet door, but Michael's clothing was hanging there. She opened the second one, but there was nothing inside.

"Where are my clothes?" she asked.

Michael paused before responding. He was so preoccupied with fixing the shed and convincing Vanessa to be his wife that he neglected to get her some clothes.

What kind of idiot am I? In hushed tones, Michael chastised himself.

"I'm sorry. Your clothes are in another room," he said.

Vanessa arched her brow as she followed him into the next room. Michael opened an old cabinet belonging to his mother. He didn't have the heart to get rid of her clothes. He could not bring himself to do so.

He took a pair of multi-colored shorts, a white T-shirt, and a few unopened pairs of underwear his mother never wore. Michael handed them to Vanessa.

"Why don't you freshen up? The bathroom's in there," he said, pointing off to the right.

Vanessa raised her brow again.

"What are my clothes doing here? How come they weren't in our room alongside yours?"

Michael had run out of excuses to justify himself. He was on the verge of insanity as he tried to come up with reasons for everything.

"We were planning to paint your closet, and you moved your clothes to this room. Because of your accident, we never had time to get started."

It struck him as a brilliant idea. Michael was satisfied with his answer.

Vanessa nodded, as if she understood. She examined the garments Michael had given her. When Vanessa asked no more questions, Michael exhaled a sigh of relief. He was grateful for her mother's clothing, because it appeared to suit Vanessa well.

Michael spoke too soon. Vanessa was at it again. She swung the cabinet wide.

"Why do these clothes remind me of my grandmother?" Vanessa asked, although she wasn't sure if she had one. She then smelled the garments. "How come it smells like musty, old moth balls?"

Michael couldn't take it any longer. Vanessa's million questions were excruciating. He had given up. Michael was prepared to confess and tell Vanessa that everything was a ruse. He simply wanted her to stop interrogating him about petty matters. Michael would return her to Honolulu, and he would return to his normal lonely life. He swallowed hard again, but Vanessa apologized before he could speak.

"I'm sorry, Michael. It's just that it's so difficult when I remember nothing about myself."

"It's OK," he said, relieved.

"Do you mind if I take a shower? I've been in the hospital for a long time, and I'm desperate for a bath."

Michael nodded and released a sense of relief as he exited the room.

Whoa! That was a stressful conversation, he murmured as he wiped the perspiration from his face.

Vanessa removed all her clothing, except for her underwear, and placed it in the laundry basket. She was looking for something to wrap around her body when Michael walked in without knocking, holding a clean towel.

"I'm sorry, I forgot to put a fresh towel in the bathroom," he apologized, and then he looked up and what a sight it was.

"Oh my God!" he said as he dropped the towel on the floor and saw Vanessa standing half-naked in front of him. Michael had lost his concentration. His mind fell into a state of lockdown. The sight of her in her underpants in front of him shocked him. But Michael couldn't take his gaze away. He attempted not to look, but it was difficult, since she was flawless in every aspect. He exited the room, but he collided with a wall, causing him to lose his footing and tumble to the floor.

"I'm sorry. I'm very sorry," Michael kept apologizing. He attempted to get up, look away, down, up, and everywhere. "I promise I saw nothing," Michael said, adding another white lie to the long list of falsehoods he couldn't remember anymore. Her beauty was hypnotic, and her perfume was seductive, even though she had just left the hospital.

Vanessa grew alarmed when she noticed Michael's cheeks growing scarlet.

"Are you OK?" she asked, attempting to help him get up. Michael couldn't do anything except sigh and lean back into her embrace.

"I'm OK," Michael murmured as he tried to stand up, but his hand did not leave her waist.

Michael and Vanessa both bent to pick up the towel. They unintentionally bumped heads, leaving Vanessa stunned and suffering from a concussion because of the unforeseen event.

"I'm so sorry," he stumbled for words.

Michael was putting Vanessa to bed when he caught a whiff of her sweet breath and couldn't stop himself. He leaned forward and kissed her lips many times. The soft contact of her mouth sent a tingling sensation through him all the way to his feet. He was delighted and brimming with desire. Michael then stepped back and let her go. He had come dangerously close to making love to her.

This is not happening. It's wrong. Remember, this is a pretend marriage to teach Vanessa a lesson. Don't mess it up, he chided himself.

Michael dashed out the door, sat on the balcony, and felt silly. He didn't want Vanessa to suspect anything was wrong. Michael returned to the room to apologize for kissing her, but his knees were trembling. Since the minute he met Vanessa, it had haunted him with apprehension. It took him some time to get a handle on himself.

Meanwhile, Vanessa watched Michael leave, but was surprised by his reaction. If she hadn't known better, she would have assumed her "husband" was uncomfortable staring at her undressed.

I believe our marriage is in danger. He couldn't even look at me with a straight face.

She sighed and shook her head, unsure whether her suspicions were correct. But the kiss seemed familiar to her, a peculiar emotion she couldn't quite pin down.

Michael felt uneasy as he prepared for bed after supper. He was sitting down pretending to read a newspaper. Vanessa stepped out of the bathroom and laid down next to him. She switched to the other side and didn't see that Michael was sweating profusely. Michael couldn't get Vanessa's lovely physique out of his head after seeing it. He stood up and grabbed a pillow.

Vanessa, perplexed, asked, "Where are you going?"

"I think it's better if I sleep in the next room."

Vanessa didn't protest and simply nodded. She exhaled a breath of relief. For a moment, it worried her. She didn't know how to tell Michael without hurting his feelings that she wanted to sleep alone, at least until she regained her memories.

Many days had passed, and although Michael was a phony husband, he looked after Vanessa as she recovered from her wounds. Before heading out to sea, he made sure Vanessa had food on the table, and even washed and changed the dressings on her head.

Vanessa's bandage was removed a few weeks later, and Dr. Phillips informed her she was healing quickly. There was no trace of any cuts or bruises from the accident. It remains to be seen if Vanessa would restore her lost memories.

CHAPTER NINE

Michael was uptight and shy before meeting Vanessa, and even though he denied it, her presence made him more comfortable and easygoing. He didn't realize he whistled and hummed a tune at home, and even when he was out at sea fishing.

Meanwhile, Vanessa saw the emotional gap between them and suspected there was a problem with their marriage. She felt alone and uneasy about their existence as a married couple, perplexed that their conversation had dried up, as if they had nothing to say. The hardest thing was that she believed Michael had lost interest in her. After their minor mishap in the bedroom when he kissed her when they head bumped, he never tried to kiss her again, or attempted to sleep with her. She couldn't fathom any actual closeness between them, and she questioned how they got that way when she knew the love was still there. She could feel him watching her, desiring her, but something was holding him back. Because of her amnesia, she realized she had a tough time starting her new life with Michael. It was a difficult transition for both of them, but she was optimistic that things would improve between them.

"Vanessa, you are now feeling better; maybe it's time you assisted me with our business," Michael said, interrupting her deep thought. He decided it was time to execute his plan before he fell apart in front of her.

"And what business is it again?" Vanessa asked, a smile on her face. She was attempting to be as nice as possible.

"Remember, I told you I'm a fisherman? I make my living by catching fish. I'll leave early in the morning, but you must make my breakfast and lunch."

Vanessa nodded and grinned. That was simple enough, she thought.

"Got it!" she said as she gave a thumbs up.

To play his part well, Michael showed Vanessa how to work around the kitchen. He cooked their supper, and Vanessa helped by setting the table, but she felt as if she had never done it before. She washed the dishes after dinner, but became frustrated as she puzzled why the plates and glasses were sliding from her grasp and breaking a few.

I feel as if I've never done this before in my life. Vanessa said as she picked up the shattered glass, pricked her fingers on the jagged edge and crying out.

Michael heard what Vanessa had said. He cracked a cheeky grin.

"Don't forget to wake up at three in the morning to prepare my food," he yelled.

Vanessa frowned as she twisted her head to look at him.

"Three o'clock in the morning?" she repeated, her tone louder than normal.

Is he insane?

Her voice didn't escape his notice. Michael grinned.

It's time to retaliate. I'll have fun with you, Vanessa, he laughed to himself.

•• ❧ ••

THE NIGHT FLEW BY. Vanessa was fast asleep as Michael shook her back and forth with a mischievous look on his face.

"Wake up, Vanessa. It's time to prepare my food."

Vanessa opened her eyes and blinked a few times. Michael was standing over her, his lips wide, shrieking something at her. She pulled herself out of bed, sat down, and stood up. Vanessa crept toward the bathroom, pushing the door open. She splashed water on her face to rouse herself awake, and rubbed it dry with a towel. For a time, Michael smiled as he watched her struggle.

Vanessa entered the kitchen while still dressed in her pajamas and bathrobe. She took the kettle to boil water for the coffee, but she stood there staring at the stove for a few minutes, since she didn't know how to operate it. Michael neglected to show her how. The burner lit after turning the knob. She smiled. She figured it out on her own.

Vanessa opened the refrigerator door and discovered an unusually shaped hot dog. She read the label: "Portuguese Sausage." Vanessa pulled it from the plastic package and placed it in a Tupperware for Michael's lunch. She filled the thermos with hot water and opened a jar of instant coffee. Vanessa poured half of it and stirred it before closing the lid. Vanessa found a loaf of Sweet Hawaiian Bread and placed it on the table for his breakfast. She poured ten tablespoons of instant coffee into a mug, added three tablespoons of sugar, filled it with hot water, and swirled it with a spoon until the instant coffee dissolved. Vanessa remembered she forgot to put sugar on the thermos, so she opened the canister and added five scoops of sugar. She had to wipe the table when the thermos spewed its contents all over the place.

Michael had finished preparing his fishing equipment. He found Vanessa sitting at the dining table. Her eyes were closed, as if she was sleeping. He sat opposite her, got a slice of bread, and smeared butter on it. He took the coffee mug off the table and blew on it. Then he took a drink, but spit it out, since the taste was awful.

"Did you put instant coffee in the mug?" he asked irritably.

Vanessa blinked open her eyes, taken aback by Michael's angry tone. She glanced at him for a moment, perplexed and disoriented.

"Vanessa, are you awake?" Michael asked again, his gaze locked on her.

Vanessa blinked many times, realizing she'd fallen asleep. "Mmm, yes?" she murmured and looked around.

"Did you use the entire jar of instant coffee in the mug?"

"Did I—did I do it wrong?" she questioned, her voice sluggish and soft.

"Well, yes," he said. "This coffee tastes terrible. You simply need one or two tablespoons of instant coffee in a cup."

"I'm sorry, Michael. I didn't know. In that case, I'll need to make some fresh coffee for your thermos." Vanessa's face flushed as she apologized.

Michael observed how uncomfortable Vanessa was and consoled her like a caring husband, telling her he would show her how to make a better cup of coffee the next time. He looked at the wall clock and knew he was late. Michael double-checked his fishing gear, making sure he had forgotten nothing. As he walked out the door, he asked Vanessa if his lunch was ready. She nodded and handed him his lunch bag. Michael, intrigued, opened it, and when he saw the Portuguese sausage inside the Tupperware, he laughed so hard that his sides hurt.

"Vanessa, I can't eat this. You must first cook it. Slice it and pan fry it. Use the same pan to make scrambled eggs for extra flavor. That is a perfect meal for me."

Vanessa learned that being a housewife was more difficult than she expected. She pulled out a pan, turned on the heat, sliced the Portuguese sausage as Michael instructed, and cooked it, but she burned herself and shouted out. Vanessa took a deep breath before cracking eggs into a glass bowl, picking out the shells, and scrambling them, but she scraped the cooked egg off of a frying pan. Cooked or not, she placed it in Michael's lunch box.

Good Lord. You'd think a mature person could cook an egg without burning it, Michael thought to himself, shaking his head as he watched her.

"Thank you," Michael murmured as Vanessa handed him his meal.

Vanessa grinned. "It's burned, but I think it's OK."

"Don't worry, I'm sure it's fine. Well, I have to leave now or I won't catch any fish," he remarked, as he walked away without kissing her.

Vanessa followed him.

"Do you want me to accompany you?"

For a time, Michael stood still at the front door. He wasn't expecting it. He didn't expect Vanessa to offer to go with him so soon. Michael quietly grinned to himself.

This may be a good thing. I believe my strategy will be successful. By George, I believe this will truly work.

"All right, if you want to," he replied, his face straight and his voice toneless.

Vanessa changed her clothing. They walked to the boat, which smelled like a rotting fish in the interior.

"Eww. What's that odor?" Vanessa asked, her nose wrinkled.

"What smell? I smell nothing," Michael said.

Vanessa furrowed her nose again.

"I have this strange hunch that I dislike fish."

"You had a horrific sea experience. Perhaps getting back into fishing is the remedy."

"Maybe you're right. All right, let's get going," Vanessa said with a smile.

Michael untied the mooring rope, hopped into the stern, and started the motor, carefully pulling away from the dock. For a moment, they appeared to be a conventional, happy, picture-perfect family, and for some strange reason, Vanessa's presence brought them good fortune. Fish almost leaped into their boat. The smell didn't bother Vanessa anymore, and she was handling the fish fine. As they returned to shore, a fish jumped out of the water and struck Vanessa as she sat in the boat. Michael came to her rescue and checked to see whether she was all right.

"Don't worry, I'm OK," Vanessa responded as she attempted to stand. "But I can't say the same about this fish."

Vanessa scooped up what she believed was a dead fish, but it startled her once it came alive in her hands. She shrieked in fear as the fish moved about in her hands, forcing her to drop it on the floor and back onto Michael, knocking him off balance. They both slipped and plunged into the water. Fortunately, Michael was an experienced swimmer and brought an unconscious Vanessa back aboard the boat safely.

Michael pulled up to the dock and jumped out. He took up a length of rope and tied the boat together. Michael walked off the dock carrying a still unconscious Vanessa. He put her in the back seat of his truck and drove off. He changed her into dry clothing and put her to bed as soon as they arrived home. Michael went outside, pacing. He was at a loss as to what to do. It had been several minutes, and Vanessa was still not waking up. He approached the bed, nervous and terrified.

"Wake up, Vanessa."

He called to her several times, but she did not move. Michael was getting worried. He took her arm and shook her.

"Wake up, please!" he screamed.

"Yeah, yeah, nag, nag. You don't have to shout," said Vanessa. She grinned at him teasingly.

Michael smiled back and touched the tip of her nose. He covered her with a light blanket and watched as she fell asleep. Moments later, he smacked himself on the head when he realized he had changed Vanessa's clothes without thinking... looking. Did he regret missing out on the opportunity to see her beautiful body again?

From then on, their relationship was better. Michael looked forward to coming home, and Vanessa couldn't wait to see him. She still struggled to learn how to cook, but she was getting better at it each day. Vanessa hummed when she cleaned; she sang when she fed the animals; and Vanessa couldn't stop smiling when she was gardening. Vanessa damaged a few clothes in the washer, but she was getting better at doing laundry. And even though her back and feet ached and her hands had blisters from the hard work, she felt content.

· · ⚬ᴏᴄ · ·

MICHAEL WAS OUT AT sea, attempting to catch fish with his net. He flung it out and hauled it back. Michael wasn't doing a good job. He didn't catch a single fish because he couldn't get Vanessa's face out of his head. Everything about her was pleasant, which puzzled him. Her beauty had left an indelible impression on him. Michael couldn't bear the thought of losing her. When he thought of her, his heart still fluttered with happiness and excitement. He tried to ignore it and focus on fishing, but he was in denial. Michael had been resisting it for a long time, but he was feeling something for her. He could deceive others, but he couldn't deny the phenomena of love at first sight to himself. Yes. He fell in love with her the moment he saw her, the day she almost hit him with her automobile. All Michael could think of after that was Vanessa. He'd never seen anyone like her before. She was harsh and opinionated, but she had a great pair of legs.

Wait! Did I say a great set of legs? I mean, she's got a terrific physique. No, I meant she has a fantastic personality. Michael's brain went into lockdown. Everything about her was new and enticing. *I miss Vanessa.*

He became excited about being with her suddenly. He turned the boat around to return to the dock. When he noticed an attractive young surfer outside their house as he walked home, his joy faded into a scowl. As he came closer, he saw it was his cousin Raul. He returned from a vacation to see his sister in New York, talking to Vanessa, who was crouching down, gardening and watering plants.

"Come on. If you don't know how to surf, I'll teach you. A gorgeous girl like you should be outside, not indoors. I'll introduce you to some of my lady friends around here."

Vanessa struggled to find the right words. This man's extra attention was charming, but was he trying to flirt with her?

Raul was now standing close to her.

"Vanessa?" He called out her name.

"Yes?" Vanessa asked as she stepped away. Raul's presence made her uncomfortable.

"May I ask you to dinner tomorrow night?"

Vanessa looked up at him, dissatisfied with the direction their conversation was heading. Raul, reaching for her hand, surprised her, but she drew it back. She attempted to ignore his far-too-pushy signals.

"I'm sorry. I should go back inside. Michael should be home any minute."

After hearing their conversation, Michael was furious.

What the hell is going on? Raul is trying to hit on my wife!

"Ahem," Michael said, clearing his throat.

He received no response.

"Ahem, ahem," he tried again, louder this time. "Excuse me, are you lost, Raul?"

"Hey, cousin, how have you been? I was just gone a few weeks, and you didn't tell me you had a gorgeous lady living in your house."

Michael scowled. His eyes expanded.

"Um, Vanessa, would you mind going inside the house, please?"

"Okay, so I'll be inside if you need me," Vanessa responded, shocked to see Michael home so early. "It was nice to meet you, Raul," she said before leaving.

Michael gave Raul an irritated glance when Vanessa entered the house.

"What do you think you're doing?"

"Are you okay, Michael? Are you mad at me? I was looking for you, and I didn't expect a beautiful young lady to open the door for me. Do you mind introducing me? She's attractive."

"I'm sorry, Raul. Did I neglect to tell you? She's my wife!" Michael said, exasperated.

"Your wife? Since when? I didn't know you got married!" he said, surprised.

"Well, I—" he paused. "Now you know, and I'd like it if you didn't hit on Vanessa, OK?"

"I'm sorry, Michael. I didn't know. Nobody on the island knew you had a girlfriend, let alone that you were married. We mistook her for a friend visiting you from the mainland. Just relax, okay?"

Michael let out a sigh and nodded his head.

"OK, cuz. I'd best leave immediately. I'll leave you two lovebirds alone," Raul laughed. "Please convey my apologies for my prior hostile actions to Vanessa. Maybe one day you'll tell me how you met."

Michael nodded again and waved to his cousin. When he was alone, he questioned why he had acted irrationally. Raul had been his cousin and best friend since childhood. He yelled at him for the first time. Why did it bother him when other guys flirted with Vanessa? He didn't like it when she chatted with other men.

What is the matter with me? Is it possible that I was jealous? No, I'm simply worried about her. Yes, I'm just concerned. Michael admitted, trying to convince himself.

His emotional struggle ruined the idea of spending quiet time with Vanessa. He was still wired and enraged.

I need to relax. I need to get a handle on myself, or I will fall apart.

.. ❧ ..

"JEALOUS MUCH?" VANESSA interrupted Michael's thoughts. He was standing on the balcony, staring at the moon.

"Huh? What? Did you say something?"

"I said, are you jealous?"

"Jealous of whom?"

"I don't know. Perhaps the person from earlier this morning. Raul, was it?"

"No, I'm not jealous. Why should I?"

"Action is more powerful than words. Sometimes it's necessary to concede defeat. You should try it once in a while," Vanessa replied, dissatisfied. She was hoping Michael would say he was jealous and tell her he loved her. She needed to hear it.

Michael was too scared to admit it. Throughout dinner, he kept silent to avoid eye contact with Vanessa. Everything affected and worried him, but he didn't know how to tell her. He was on the balcony when Vanessa invited him to go for a walk on the beach. Michael, who had been trying all night to avoid Vanessa, instantly consented. He leaped at the chance to be with her alone, and he wasn't about to allow a minor incident with Raul to ruin his time with Vanessa. Michael was no longer concerned about the consequences. He felt the beach was the ideal setting for an intimate moment, gazing at the moon and stars and listening to the waves roll by.

Before heading out to the beach with Vanessa, Michael grabbed a blanket and a bottle of champagne. They strolled hand in hand, listening to the waves and letting them wash over their bare feet. When the water reached her shins, Vanessa groaned.

They'd been walking for a while when Michael stopped at his favorite spot. It wasn't far, and when they got there, they sat on the trunk of a coconut tree that had fallen on the beach after a storm, and drank champagne while talking. The sky, moon, and stars glowed and left light streaks that stretched forever over the water. Vanessa felt cold as the breeze blew across their hair. Michael wrapped a blanket around her and held her in his arms as if he were protecting her. Vanessa relished the tingling sensations it provided her as she rested her head against his shoulder and looked into Michael's eyes.

I am confident that there is yet hope for us. Whatever is preventing Michael from getting close to me, we can still figure it out.

And she was right. Michael leaned forward and kissed her softly, teasing in its intention and surprising even himself that he could be so forward. To his surprise, Vanessa kissed him back. She feared that if she didn't kiss him right away, he'd go insane. Michael responded in kind. He deepened the kiss as if he longed to explore every inch of her. They kissed until both of them were gasping for air. Vanessa and Michael both stared out at the water, sometimes glancing at each other. Before they returned home, Michael kissed her on the cheek. He realized that the closer he got to Vanessa, the more difficult it would be to suppress his sexual desires. Since the first moment he laid eyes on her, he had longed to make love to her. Michael wasn't sure how long he could control himself now that Vanessa was getting close to him.

If only Michael knew how Vanessa felt. Vanessa believed they were truly married. It was difficult for her to accept at first, and she was miserable, but she believed in the sacredness of marriage and the obligation to respect lifelong promises. Vanessa did not know what that meant. She heard on the radio the other day that marriage was a long-term commitment. Although she enjoyed the little things Michael did for her, she often pondered what had transpired between them before her accident. She wasn't sure if their marriage was falling apart or if he had fallen out of love because he had stopped making love to her. She admitted that when Michael moved out of their bedroom and told her it was better to sleep in different rooms until she regained her memory, Vanessa felt it was a great idea then. But it had been a while, and she hopes they had become closer by now. If their marriage was in trouble, he sent her conflicting signals, but she remained optimistic.

I'm not going down without a fight in our marriage. It's clear that it's up to me to make it work.

CHAPTER TEN

Vanessa had become a typical Towi Island housewife. She learned how to cook, clean the house, do the laundry, and operate household appliances. She was acclimating to the island's way of life, which endeared her to Michael even more.

On his way home from an overnight fishing trip, Michael met a group of attractive young women. Sherice and Sheryl were two of his childhood friends. They had moved to Honolulu two years ago, along with their other sister, Sharon, and had rented an apartment together. They returned home for a week of vacation.

"We're having a get-together tonight, Michael. You should come. We'll make your favorite dish and have a case of beer waiting for you," the sisters said.

Meanwhile, Vanessa had arranged a surprise meal for Michael using a different dish she had discovered on her own. Michael was a big fan of coconut-flavored foods. She prepared the chicken using coconut milk and was pleased with how it turned out. Vanessa couldn't wait for Michael to try her latest dish. When she heard his voice outside, she went to greet him, only to stop at the door when she saw a group of young women flirting with him. She couldn't believe Michael seemed to flirt back. There was a tinge of jealousy near her heart.

When Michael walked into the house, he was greeted with the aroma of coconut. The smell flooded the kitchen. He noticed a medium-sized pot on the stove and opened it with eagerness; it was his favorite dish: chicken in coconut milk.

I'm curious about what this will taste like this time.

Vanessa tried several cooking techniques, but it was the chicken with coconut milk recipe that gave her difficulties. She'd tried countless times previously to perfect it, but they all tasted terrible.

"This is a great treat, Vanessa," he remarked, smiling. "Where are you?"

Michael yelled out to her many times, but she did not respond. He checked in the bedroom, the bathroom, and the living area, but couldn't find Vanessa. He looked in the front and backyard, but there was no sign of her.

Michael went to Sophia's house, his seventy-year-old next-door neighbor. He saw her as his second mother. He asked whether she had seen Vanessa. Sophia wagged her fingers at him, shouting and chastising him for flirting with other women.

"You're a jerk. Why would you flirt when you have a beautiful wife waiting for you at home?"

"What are you talking about, Sophia? Have you seen Vanessa? Do you know where she is? Please tell me. I'm worried."

"It serves you right. Do you know what your wife did today? She slaved tirelessly to prepare your favorite meal, hoping to impress you with her cooking skills, but you surprised her by flirting with other girls."

Michael's lips twitched slightly. Vanessa grew jealous when she saw him conversing with his female friends.

"No, Sophia, that is not what happened. Where is she? Please, I need to talk with her," he said.

Sophia let out a long sigh.

"Vanessa, come on out. Your husband has something to tell you."

But Vanessa refused to come out, so Michael went into Sophia's room and found her weeping on the edge of the bed. Her shoulders trembled.

"I'm sorry, Vanessa. I didn't flirt with anyone. Honest! Please believe me. Those women you saw me speak to earlier are sisters. We've known each other since we were little kids. They're like my sisters to me, nothing more. Please believe me."

Vanessa brushed her tears away.

"Seriously? You weren't flirting with them?" She braced herself to hear the answer.

"My wife is ten times more attractive than they are, so why would I look at anyone else?"

Vanessa giggled when she heard it. She hugged him, and Michael couldn't stop himself from embracing her back. They reconciled, and after explaining everything to Sophia, Vanessa apologized for the trouble she had created. Sophia accepted her apologies and waved as they walked away.

When they arrived home, Vanessa laid the table for them to dine.

"I'll cook. Give me a minute, and I'll have something ready for us," Michael said.

"No, silly. I made dinner. Just watch TV or something," Vanessa said as she shoved him toward the living room.

"Well, if you say so, but remember, if you need help, I'm only a room away," Michael joked.

Vanessa nodded and pushed him out of the kitchen. The table was quickly set, and the meal was ready.

"Let's eat," Vanessa said. "I'm famished."

Michael could smell the wonderful scent of the evening's meal. He paused at the doorway, staring at the food. The chicken with coconut milk on a platter looked appetizing, but Michael was skeptical. He grumbled as he sliced a little piece, took a taste, and declared it delicious. Michael had to admit that Vanessa's many experiments with various dishes had paid off. He spooned some steaming rice onto his plate and placed an enormous quantity of chicken over it. As he chewed the meal, he imagined he was in heaven.

Vanessa enjoyed watching her husband devour everything she had prepared. Despite several failures in the kitchen, she considered it a miracle that she had learned to cook. Michael attempted to speak twice with his mouth full, but Vanessa told him to be quiet and eat first. Between bites, Michael mentioned to Vanessa that the sisters had asked them to attend a get-together at their home.

"They are here for a visit, and we haven't seen each other in a long time. Is it okay for us to go?"

Vanessa rolled her eyes. She didn't want to see those females flirt with Michael again, but she also didn't want to feel as if she was suffocating him. Even though her heart was screaming "no," she pretended everything was OK, and she said she was glad to meet his friends.

· · ᴏᴥᴏ · ·

THERE WERE MANY PEOPLE at the party. Vanessa thought it was a small dinner gathering with only Michael and her. She saw a good-looking woman talking animatedly with a group of young men while sipping wine. Seeing the woman laugh and move seductively made Vanessa shudder.

She's a fraud.

When she spotted the woman approaching them, she grimaced.

"Hello, Michael," Sharon said as she kissed him on the cheeks. She wrapped her arms around him, but when she noticed Vanessa, she arched an eyebrow. "And who is this lady with you?"

"Sharon, meet Vanessa, my wife," Michael said.

It surprised Sharon, causing her to cough on her drink.

"Y-your wife?" she stutters. "I did not know you got married."

"Yeah, we're newlyweds," Michael replied, as he put his arm around Vanessa's.

Sharon studied Vanessa from head to toe, looking for flaws. She looked at her intently and couldn't believe her flawless beauty—she was practically perfect. The only defect she could perceive was that she was too sweet, but she knew deep down that it wasn't a flaw at all.

Meanwhile, Vanessa looked up to see Sharon watching her; her face was stolid, although her glance acknowledged her presence. It relieved her that they didn't have to speak. Something about this woman made her jealous.

"Would you mind staying after the party, Michael? I have things I want to give you," Sharon said, wrapping her arms around his again and lifting her eyebrows at Vanessa.

"Yes. Vanessa and I will stay for a while," Michael said.

Vanessa wrapped her arms around her husband's other side and raised an eyebrow, saying, "Yes, my husband and I will stay awhile."

Sharon returned her attention to Vanessa, who met her gaze boldly.

That scheming little witch! Sharon thought to herself as she headed to the wine table. She took a glass and drank it.

.. ⚜ ..

EVERYONE ADMIRED THE young couple at the party as they heated up on the dance floor. Vanessa was dressed casually in a black dress and an inch-high sandal, but she looked stunning. Michael beamed. He was proud to show off his wife.

Sharon was still standing near the wine table, having had far too many alcoholic beverages. It enraged her when she saw Michael dancing with Vanessa. She couldn't accept he had married. Sharon thought she and Michael had a special relationship, even though Michael had never asked her out. She expected them to end up together and marry someday. Sharon didn't waste time when she saw Vanessa walking to the bathroom. She walked over to Michael and openly flirted with him. Michael had known Sharon for a long time and knew she was just playing around. He missed the clue that she was interested in him. Perhaps because he only saw her as a sister, and nothing more.

"Sharon, you're drunk. What's the matter with you?" Michael asked.

"Come on, Michael, dance with me," Sharon slurred.

"You've had too much to drink, Sharon."

Sherice and Sheryl, who were busy serving food on a tray, saw that everyone was staring at their sister, making a fool of herself. They went up to her, grabbed her arms, and dragged her to her room, despite Sharon's protests. Vanessa was returning from the restroom when she witnessed the entire incident.

When she approached Michael, she whispered in his ear. "She's got the hots for you, Michael. I overheard several individuals discussing it. They knew Sharon had a thing for you for years, and for some strange reason, you missed it."

"No way!" said Michael. "Sharon is a close friend. That's all."

"If you say so," Vanessa replied, smiling.

"Don't tell me you're jealous again," Michael joked.

"I trust you," she answered. "Sharon? I'm not sure."

Vanessa's voice was low, but loud enough for Michael to know she had feelings for him. He felt a surge of joy inside himself. He sighed and seized the opportunity. Michael gazed into Vanessa's eyes and touched her cheek. He could no longer conceal the natural desires that surged through him. Michael could no longer fight his feelings and could not resist putting his arms around her body. He kissed her with a fiery passion that had been simmering for a long time.

Vanessa could not resist; his caresses sent her reeling into submission. She wanted him as much as he wanted her. They kissed, and Vanessa savored his possessive touches. They were in the midst of a tender moment when Raul interrupted their somewhat compromising position.

"Good evening, lovebirds!"

Raul had taken them completely by surprise. Michael and Vanessa knew others were watching at them. Applause erupted around the room. Vanessa was mortified, and her cheeks flushed scarlet, but not Michael. He waited for the cheering to subside. Michael turned around to make eye contact with everyone as the chatter died down. He cleared his throat to regain everyone's attention.

"Friends, please meet my lovely wife, Vanessa!" he stated.

Cheers erupted again when Michael threw his arms around Vanessa and kissed her on the lips in front of everyone. Vanessa cleared her throat and greeted everyone, her voice shaking. Michael clapped his hands. He seems captivated, even proud of her. He grasped her hand in his, and they danced to the beat of their hearts. Everyone burst out laughing, and the cheering went on. Vanessa had a good time. She seemed pleased and content for the first time.

· · ༄ · ·

THE GATHERING FINISHED at midnight. Except for family members and the two sisters who were cleaning up, everyone had gone home. Michael and Vanessa also decided it was time to leave.

"Where's Sharon?" asked Michael when Sherice came to see him. "She told us to wait after the party. She had things to give me."

"I'm sorry, Michael, but she's resting in bed. I'm not sure why she drank so much tonight." Sherice expressed concern over this. "It's not like her to do something like this."

"Just tell her we waited, but now we have to go home. We'll see her when she's feeling better," Michael added.

Vanessa heard what Michael had said. She wished to voice her displeasure. Sharon was the person she wanted to see the least of all. Even worse, she did not want Michael to see her again. Vanessa had been watching Sharon from across the room the whole night, and it was clear: Sharon wanted Michael!

"Sherice, would you mind checking Sharon's room to see whether she packed whatever she wanted to give to Michael? He'll be at sea first thing tomorrow morning, and she might not see him. We'll take it with us if it's ready. Is that all right?"

"I don't see any reason why not! I'm going to check on her room now."

Sherice emerged a few minutes later, carrying a little box with Michael's name written on the cover. There were boxes of chocolate macadamia nuts and packs of Kona coffee inside. Sheryl gave it to Michael.

Michael and Vanessa walked home in silence until he couldn't take it any longer and asked.

"Vanessa, please tell me the truth. Are you jealous of the sisters? I've never seen you act like that before. Does this suggest you're in love with me?" he asked.

"What do you mean if I'm in love with you?" she said. "I'm married to you. Of course, I'm madly in love with you. Sometimes you amaze me with your method of questioning."

Michael realized he had said something incorrectly. He kissed Vanessa on the lips just as she was about to become suspicious.

"I'm sorry. I was simply playing with you," he explained.

"Michael, Sharon is stunning, and it's clear she has feelings for you. How come you didn't hook up with her?"

Michael came to a halt. He drew her chin up to meet his stare.

"I don't like it when a woman throws herself at me. I like to seduce rather than be seduced." Michael kissed her on the lips and whispered, "Now that I'm married, the only person I'll seduce is you." He did a good job of playing the role of a devoted husband.

Vanessa pinched her husband. She smiled like a giddy schoolgirl as she thought to herself, "This man is so adorable."

CHAPTER ELEVEN

Sharon went to see Michael the next day. She wanted to clear things up between them. She knew she had made a fool of herself. Sharon cautiously knocked and waited. Vanessa took some time to open the door. Sharon's presence surprised her, and she paused for a moment to reflect.

"If you're looking for Michael, he's not here," she explained. "You just missed him, and he won't be back till later. Would you like to join me for some refreshments?" Vanessa invited her in.

Sharon entered the house, walked into the living room, and sat down, feeling uneasy. Vanessa broke the stillness before she could say anything.

"Sharon, I'm glad you came, because I wanted to talk to you. Something has been bothering me."

Sharon was nervous and uncomfortably seated next to Vanessa. She already knew what she was going to ask her. She knew that she had ruined everything by revealing her actual feelings for Michael at the party the night before.

"W-what do you want to ask me?" She stuttered.

Vanessa took a deep breath before speaking.

"I'll go straight to the point, Sharon. Do you have feelings for my husband? I apologize if I'm mistaken, but based on your behavior last night, I believe you do."

Sharon felt tears welling up in her eyes and attempted to keep them hidden. Sharon's face flushed with rage, her eyes bulging, and her lips drawn in a harsh line as she raised her head and noticed Vanessa staring suspiciously at her. Vanessa was correct in her assessment. She was madly in love with Michael. She thought Michael felt the same way about her. Although they hadn't spoken since she moved to Honolulu, she was certain Michael was merely playing hard to get.

How could he do this to me?

Sharon's animosity and loathing became deeper, and she nearly burst into tears. She focused her attention on Vanessa. Sharon couldn't think of anything negative to say about her. She was perfect. She resented her. Sharon stood up.

"Just let Michael know I dropped by."

"Wait a minute, Sharon!" Vanessa shouted out to her, but Sharon slammed the front door behind her as she dashed home, not looking back.

Vanessa was pacing back and forth in the living room, undecided on what to do. Sharon had to end her feelings for Michael. Her marriage needs to be saved. She got dressed and went to Sharon's place. Sherice opened the door and informed her that Sharon had taken the last ferry back to Honolulu.

Vanessa exhaled a breath of relief. Sharon made the wise decision to leave Towi Island for the good of everyone.

This town is too small for both of us.

• • ⚓ • •

VANESSA BECAME A SERIOUS cook after the success of her chicken with coconut milk, and she was not afraid to try new things. She simply needed a confidence boost. Vanessa enjoyed cooking for Michael. She created recipes, developed new ideas, cooking skills, and techniques. Michael and Sophia were her test subjects for her cuisine. Much to Vanessa's delight, many of her friends, who dubbed her "Island Master Chef," quickly loved her unique dishes. Vanessa got more inspired to try different recipes because of Michael's encouragement, and after a while, she preferred to be at home cooking rather than out on the sea fishing. She launched a small catering business, which was an instant success. Michael provided the fish, and she prepared it.

Vanessa and Michael couldn't be happier. She became an outstanding role model for young girls when she volunteered at the hospital. Vanessa's transition to a better person than she had been in her prior life shocked Michael. She could trudge through it all, and there was no evidence of her spoiled habits.

Michael's guilt grew as time went on. He knew what he had done was wrong, and repeatedly tried to tell Vanessa the truth, but he couldn't figure out what to say. Michael was afraid of losing her if he spoke the truth. He was madly, deeply in love with her. Vanessa was the best thing that ever happened to him.

Vanessa sat down next to Michael on the balcony one night.

"I know it's been a long time since we've been intimate, you know, after the accident. And I want you to know that I've never been happier in my life than I am right now with you. I love you with all my heart, but I'm selfish and didn't consider your sentiments. I want you to be happy, Michael," Vanessa said, sobbing. She closed her eyes as Michael brushed away her tears.

Michael felt the same way, but he knew it was wrong. He pondered. He felt an unpleasant twinge of remorse twisting through him.

"Vanessa, I... um, I have something to, uh..." he stuttered. "What I'm trying to say is, well, I..."

"Michael, I'm giving you permission to kiss, hold, and make love to me. I've been meaning to tell you this for a long time. I love you, Michael, and I want to make love to you every day and forever."

It was music to Michael's ears. Oh, how he wished he could kiss Vanessa for a long time, touch her soft skin, and make love to her till morning. And he knew it was wrong. He had to keep his feelings for her in check.

I can't take advantage of Vanessa's condition. What if she regains her memory? What if she dislikes me after learning the truth?

"Michael?" Vanessa interrupted his stream of thought.

Michael glanced at Vanessa's beautiful face and the silky lips he'd been yearning to kiss. But who was he kidding? What they had was a forbidden love. He made every attempt to ignore her and turn away. Vanessa sensed his apprehension.

"I'm sorry, Michael. Did I say something wrong?" She asked, perplexed.

Michael stayed motionless. He saw no reason why things would go wrong if he told her the truth.

If she becomes furious, I shall ask her forgiveness. Vanessa is a kind person. The old Vanessa is long gone. I'm confident she'll come around to forgive me.

Michael felt justified in assuming that after everything they'd been through together, she'd forgiven him. Meanwhile, the cold air touched Vanessa's skin, making her shudder, and she dashed back inside the house to get her sweater.

Michael was left alone, distraught. He didn't know how much longer he could deny Vanessa the truth of his feelings. How could he express his love for her when he knew he had lied to her? He paced the floor. It wasn't fair to keep Vanessa in the dark anymore, but he had to wait for the right moment to tell her. He prayed she never regained her memories. He didn't want to lose her.

· · ∽ · ·

VANESSA WAS ALONE AT home on a Saturday morning, since Michael had gone on an overnight fishing trip with his buddies. Sophia was closing her door when she noticed Vanessa gardening. They started a conversation. Sophia wondered whether Vanessa would be interested in volunteering at the town's annual rummage sale, held at the community center. She stated that the City and County of Towi Island supported the town's rummage sales twice a year, in the spring and fall. Homeowners on the island combed through their closets and storage units, pulling forth treasures to sell. The purpose of this year's event was to gather funds to purchase equipment for the children's playground. Vanessa felt it was a wonderful thing for the community to do, and told Sophia it would delight her to assist. She changed and left a note for Michael when he returned.

When they arrived, there were many volunteers setting things up. Sophia and Vanessa helped set up the tables before the people arrived. They stuffed them with kitchen utensils, towels, photo frames, and decorations. Accessories such as earrings and bracelets were also on display. They dispersed the heavy objects, which included furniture, sewing machines, and gym equipment, around the parking lot. They put tags on each piece and made sure the prices were reasonable. Sophia placed additional items on the small table when she noticed a large yellow box. She browsed through it, and it was full of items that she knew Vanessa would like.

"Vanessa, come here. Look at these dresses. These are also in your size."

Vanessa giggled and dashed up to the box Sophia was rummaging in. There were outfits with matching shoes, hats, and purses.

"I'm curious who donated these," Sophia thought. "Do you want them?" she asked.

Vanessa fixed her gaze on Sophia. When she understood what was going on, she flung her arms around the elderly woman.

"Sure! Who wouldn't? They're stunning!"

"Well, choose whatever you want."

"But these are for sale to raise money. I don't feel right taking them."

Sophia paused for a while to consider her options.

"Hey, Lester, could you just come over here for a moment?"

Lester was the chairperson of the rummage sale.

"Lester, may we buy the unsold stuff when the sale is over?"

"Of course, you can. Anything you can fit in a paper bag is only $1," Lester said.

"You got a deal!" Sophia laughed as she shook Lester's hand and grinned at Vanessa.

They opened the door to the public a few moments later to begin the bargain search. There was a swarm of people waiting outside. By midday, they had sold most of their items, with only a few large objects, such as chairs and tables, remaining. Lester thanked the volunteers and informed them it was time to clean up.

Vanessa looked around, disappointed they had sold the clothing she wanted. Then she noticed a few boxes on the floor and realized they forgot to place them on the table. Vanessa opened them and discovered new sandals in her size. She tried on various colored flats and high heels. Sophia peered inside the room and saw Vanessa twirling around like a little girl. She smiled and clapped her hands to Vanessa's embarrassment.

"Don't be shy, Vanessa. You look stunning, and do you know what would complete your look?"

"What?" Vanessa asked, her eyes twinkling.

"Those dresses we saw earlier."

"But, Sophia, we sold them."

"What?" a confused Sophia asked.

Sophia exhaled with relief as she peeked into the cabinet and noticed the yellow box was still inside. Sophia hid it when Lester was not looking. She took the box from the cabinet, and when Vanessa realized what she had done, she shot her a wicked glance.

She chuckled and said, "You nasty old lady."

"Well, I'm old. Shoot me," Sophia responded, and they both laughed.

At Sophia's request, Vanessa put on a short floral pink dress and black heels. Sophia couldn't believe how beautiful Vanessa was.

"My child, you look like royalty."

"Do you think I'd pass for a beauty queen?" She laughed.

"My darling, you will pass for a queen," Sophia said.

Vanessa twirled in front of the full-length mirror, appreciating her dress. She was unaware that Michael had arrived. He crept behind the door, watching Vanessa turn. The dress highlighted the attractiveness of her appealing physique, making her appear even more lovely than before.

"Now these are my kind of clothing," Vanessa said as she returned to the room and picked out another garment to put on. This time, it was a black cocktail dress. She held it in her arms and stared at it. She put it on and it fit her perfectly.

She put on the black high-heeled shoes and twirled around again. She smiled as she collapsed on the floor. Sophia grinned at the sight of Vanessa having some fun. Michael, who was still cowering behind the door, chuckled, staring at her and shaking his head.

Oh, Vanessa. You're silly and adorable.

He decided it was time to see this beautiful woman face-to-face. Vanessa was still lying on her back, resting, and when she got up, she was surprised to see Michael standing in front of her, giving her his hand. He returned her smile. As she took hold of his hand and pulled her up, Michael lost his balance and fell right next to her, bringing her down beside him.

Sophia giggled at their slightly humorous accident. Michael smiled as he rolled over and glanced at Vanessa. She could feel his warm breath on her. Michael leaned closer, her arms around his neck, and they looked into each other's eyes.

"Ahem." Sophia cleared her voice to attract their attention.

Vanessa and Michael sprang to their feet and giggled. Michael paid for the dresses and shoes, as well as a $100 donation to the credit of the children's playground fund. He carried the boxes as they walked to the truck to return home. He kept looking in his rear-view mirror while driving, trying to catch a glimpse of Vanessa. Sophia, who was sitting in the front seat, noticed it and chuckled.

"Be careful, Michael. You may fracture your neck!" She made a remark.

"I'm sorry, Sophia," Michael replied, his cheeks flushed with embarrassment. He adjusted the rear-view mirror again and looked at Vanessa to check whether she heard Sophia's comment. When he saw her staring out the window, he breathed a sigh of relief.

If only he knew. Vanessa was pretending to look out the window because she couldn't stop giggling. She was enthralled by what she had heard. She enjoyed seeing Michael make a fool of himself.

CHAPTER TWELVE

Sophia attended her niece's wedding on the other side of the island. She asked Vanessa to come along, and Michael hesitated.

"It's only for one day, Michael. It'll give Vanessa a chance to meet other women here on the island. Don't tell me you want to come along, too?"

Michael said nothing. He remained silent.

"All right, Michael, I was only teasing you. Of course, you are coming. You're taking us there. You are our chauffeur. Just pick me up at my place at three o'clock. It is not a formal occasion, so dress casually."

Michael finally smiled. "You got it, Sophia!"

At the party, Michael had one arm around Vanessa's tiny waist in a possessive grip. Vanessa was savoring it, and she let him lead her into the room. When they walked in, all eyes were on them. Vanessa wore a short white dress that exposed her back, while Michael sported Levi's jeans, leather boots, and a white shirt that matched Vanessa's outfit.

Sophia handed Vanessa a glass of wine and then introduced her to her friends, who seemed thrilled to meet her. Vanessa did not join the chattering women; instead, she strolled outside on the balcony to take in the scenery and get some fresh air.

Meanwhile, Michael was talking with his friends, and when he glanced back at Vanessa, she was gone. When he couldn't find her, he grew concerned. He felt relieved when he saw her standing on the balcony—her beauty captured by the moonlight. Suddenly, Vanessa's wine glass slipped from her hand, spilling its content on the floor. Michael picked up the broken glass, and he saw Vanessa's long, shapely legs, and it weakened him.

Sophia observed Michael from a distance and couldn't help but notice how attentive he was to Vanessa. She sighed, puzzled why Michael was usually odd around Vanessa. He wasn't behaving like a married man, but like a hot young athlete in love with the prom queen.

What's his story?

Sophia's gaze remained fixed on them. Throughout the night, Michael never left Vanessa's side. His friends taunted him that marriage had changed him.

"Come on, Michael, join us for a drink," his friends urged.

Michael turned to Vanessa as if he asked her for permission.

She smiled, nodded, and said, "Have fun!"

"Sorry, sweetheart, my fans are waiting for me," he said, laughing, giving her a quick kiss on the lips.

"Vanessa, we'll borrow your husband for a moment. We haven't seen him in a long time," Michael's buddies exclaimed as they grabbed his arm and led him back to the bar, where they handed him a shot of glass and vodka.

Vanessa could hear Michael's pals cheering as they played shot glass roulette. She looked around at the guests. A middle-aged woman with black hair graying at the temples stood to her right. She was dressed in a yellow and pink sundress and seemed in her late forties. A young woman in her twenties was on the phone, agitatedly waving her hand in the air. Vanessa could feel the woman's blood pressure rise with every loud word. The bride looked stunning in traditional Hawaiian clothing. Her hair was long and wavy, and she wore a floral crown known as a "Haku lei," which was a lei composed of local plants and flowers. Vanessa wondered if she was as happy as she was when she got married. She pondered if she had a small wedding or an elegant one.

Vanessa caught the bride's attention as she looked at her. She realized her thoughts had wandered, and she hadn't realized she was gazing at her. She shrugged and said, "Sorry I'm staring." The bride returned her grin with a nod.

"Vanessa!" Sophia called, happy to see her. "What are you doing out on the balcony?"

"I need some fresh air. Michael will be here shortly. His friends are having a good time with him. They're teasing him because he's married."

Sophia's look shifted to curiosity. "Vanessa, is everything all right with you and Michael?"

"Never been better. Why'd you ask?"

"Nothing. I was just thinking. How long have you been married again?"

"Not long; only a few months," Vanessa said. That's what Michael had told her when she asked. "Everything between us is perfect. Simply amazing. It's as though we're still dating."

"That's exactly what I'm saying. I've known Michael since he was a child. He is shy and reserved. He's not a passionate man, and the way he talks and looks at you is strange. It's almost as though he's a different person."

"I agree, Sophia. We had a tense beginning to our marriage. We improved once we got beyond the uncomfortable period. He makes me feel special every day, and I am madly in love with him." Vanessa said, her face shining with delight.

Sophia nodded, but with trepidation. Something unusual happened to Michael. To put her theory to the test, Sophia invited Vanessa to go to town with her the next day.

• • ∽⊷∾ • •

"JUST DROP US OFF IN the mall and pick us up at noon in front of the Liberty Bell," Sophia explained.

"I'm still baffled why I can't join you."

"Keep quiet, Michael. It's a girl's day out."

"All right, Sophia. I understand! Don't get upset. I know when I'm not wanted," Michael joked. He kissed Vanessa on the cheeks before departing, and then drove away while Vanessa waved.

It was a beautiful day for shopping. Sophia not only purchased a dress she loved, but also treated herself and Vanessa to a spa treatment, a new haircut, and a pedicure and manicure. Then they went to a boutique shop and looked through the sale areas, which were stocked with racks of clothing at 50% off.

At noon, Michael waited for Sophia and Vanessa in front of the Liberty Bell. When he spotted Sophia waving at him, he took the packages from her hands and put them inside the truck.

"Where is Vanessa?" he asked.

"She'll be along. She stopped by the ladies' room."

Michael leaned against his truck, watching the passersby. A few moments later, he noticed a woman heading down the steps, her hair blowing in the wind. For a brief period, time seemed to stand still. Michael didn't recognize Vanessa because of her new hairstyle. She looked stunning, even in a tank top and pants. He opened the side door, and she slid inside, smiling. Michael pulled the seatbelt over her shoulder. He realized he was close to her, and he could smell her lovely perfume, which was intoxicating. It was a breaking point. He kissed her passionately, and Vanessa let him.

Sophia swallowed and cleared her throat. "When are we leaving, Michael?"

As soon as he realized they weren't alone in the car, Michael said, "Now, Sophia, now," attempting to get back to normal.

Vanessa sat in the rear seat, while Sophia sat in the front. Michael drove within the speed limit. He angled the rear-view mirror to get a better look at Vanessa. Tourists flocked to the small gift stores farther up the road. Michael was fixated on Vanessa and didn't notice two people crossing the street. As he slammed on the brake, his eyes widened.

Okay, that was a close call, he thought to himself. He had to concentrate on the road in front of him to avoid becoming distracted. He couldn't allow his thoughts to take control of his actions and reactions.

Michael took Vanessa and Sophia to a small Japanese restaurant for lunch. He also bought them ice cream cones, and they ate them while walking down the pier. Vanessa tried on sunglasses at a kiosk, while Sophia bought a new hat and scarf.

"How about we go dancing at the club tonight?" Sophia proposed. "It's Saturday night, and I haven't gone dancing in a long time. What do you think, Michael?"

"That's an excellent idea. Vanessa, how about it? Would you like to go dancing tonight?"

"Sure, I'm up for it if you are."

"All right, Sophia, it's a date," Michael remarked, his eyes twinkling.

"Dancing starts at eight o'clock. Take me home so I can get dressed," Sophia said.

Michael glanced at his watch. It was only six-thirty. He nodded and drove home as fast as he could. He saw it as an opportunity to spend quality time with Vanessa before they went to the club. Michael parked his truck in the driveway. He walked around to the truck's side and opened the door for Vanessa and Sophia.

"I'll see you later," Sophia remarked as she headed towards her house, waving her hand.

When Michael and Vanessa were ready to enter the house, they heard a voice calling to them. Michael turned around to see who it was, and was disappointed to realize it was his cousin, Raul.

"What brought you here, Raul?" he asked, his voice rising.

"What's with the gloomy expression?" Raul asked sarcastically. "I'm here because Uncle Bert is moving to Los Angeles and is selling his fishing gear. I immediately thought of you. He's selling it for a cheap price. I told Uncle Bert not to sell it to anyone until you had a chance to see it for yourself. So, let's get going!"

"Can I see him tomorrow? We're going dancing tonight."

"He'd want to get rid of it tonight. You don't want to miss out on a good deal, believe me."

"Why don't you go ahead, Michael? I still need to get ready. Sophia and I will wait for you at the club." Vanessa suggested.

"Are you sure?" he asked.

"Don't be silly, Sophia and I will be fine."

Before jumping into his truck and speeding off to their uncle's place, Michael kissed Vanessa goodbye. He needed to get the business done quickly, so he could go on his date with Vanessa.

·· ✤ ··

VANESSA WAS DRESSED in a white strapless dress and black strapped high heel shoes that accentuated her long legs. Sophia was clad in a Hawaiian muumuu, a beaded necklace, and a flower in her hair.

The club was packed with both locals and visitors when they arrived. Vanessa didn't believe they could get a table.

"Don't worry," Sophia said. "Before coming here, I called a friend."

As they made their way through the rear entrance, Sophia met Carlos, the bartender.

"Who is this lovely lady with you, Sophia?" he inquired.

"It's Vanessa, Michael's wife."

"Michael got married? It's about time. He found a real gem in her."

"Thank you, Carlos," Vanessa said, smiling.

"So, where is Michael?" Carlos asked.

"Oh, he'll be here soon," Sophia replied.

Carlos escorted them to a table reserved for them. As they made their way into the crowded room, everyone was taken aback by Vanessa's stunning beauty. Her loveliness was undeniable, and no one could take their eyes off her. Nobody knew who she was when they inquired.

"Could you please get us our drinks, Carlos?" Sophia asked.

Carlos nodded and returned with Mai Tais for the ladies and a beer for Michael.

"Excuse me, ladies, but may I join you?"

Vanessa and Sophia raised their heads to find a handsome young man with fair blond hair and blue eyes standing near their table.

Sophia cracked a grin.

"Well, young man, I'm all yours if you're here to pick me up!"

The good-looking stranger smiled and slid into the seat beside Sophia.

"My name is Chris," he began, shaking Sophia's hand, but his baby blue eyes were riveted on Vanessa.

Meanwhile, Michael arrived at the club. There was a long line, and he expected to see Vanessa and Sophia, but he didn't see them. He informed the bouncer that his companions were already inside, so he allowed him in. Michael sought for them, but it was too crowded for him to see. He eventually found Vanessa and made his way through the crowd. Vanessa smiled as she spotted her six-foot-two-inch gorgeous husband approaching.

Michael muttered, "Hey, gorgeous," before placing the most amazing kiss on her. "You outshine everyone here tonight."

When Vanessa introduced Michael as her husband, Chris was shocked and upset. He knew it was time for him to leave.

"I don't want to intrude," Chris whispered as he struggled to get out of his seat, his gaze fixated on Vanessa. "Good night, Sophia and Vanessa..."

Chris gave Michael a sharp look before departing.

"Who was he? Did you cause another poor soul to cry?" Michael made a lighthearted remark.

"He's a man attempting to hit on Sophia," Vanessa joked.

"Yes, Michael. He was about to make a move on me when you interrupted him."

Michael laughed as he walked to the bar to get more beer and drinks for himself and the ladies. Everyone, even Chris, felt envious of him. Michael knew that, and he couldn't blame them. Vanessa was the most attractive girl in the bar, and she was a total knockout.

"Will you dance with me?" Michael asked when he returned with their drinks.

Vanessa nodded, and he took her hand in his and led her to the dance floor.

"Did I mention how stunning you look tonight?" Michael murmured in her ear. "Did you see how many eyes are on you, wondering who this woman is?"

As they danced to the slow music, Vanessa smiled and placed her head on his shoulder.

Sophia couldn't help but grin as she watched Michael and Vanessa dance and stare into each other's eyes. All her reservations vanished. She could see now that they were genuinely in love.

CHAPTER THIRTEEN

Vanessa was seen walking around the island with Michael now that their relationship was widely known. He wanted to show her off to everyone he knew.

One morning, Michael took Vanessa shopping for new clothes. It was the village's monthly luau. He hadn't been around for their get together in a while, because Vanessa lived with him. This time, he planned to attend, and he would bring Vanessa with him. He wanted her to look her best. He wanted Vanessa to meet his friends, whom he regarded as family.

Vanessa was looking forward to returning to the town's boutique. There were racks of different colored blouses, pullover shirts, sweaters, short dresses, long dresses, blue jeans, lingerie, perfumes, and lotions. She never got weary of looking at them.

"I find shopping an amazing activity." Vanessa explained, "I believe I had a penchant for fashion in a previous life."

She picked up a few items, and Michael smiled as she put on a hat and toyed with it. But every now and then, Michael felt a stab of acute remorse. Vanessa would never go into a store like that. He was certain her expensive dresses were half the price of the town.

Vanessa chose a pink spaghetti strap mini dress with low heel strappy shoes. She tried it on, and when she walked out of the fitting room and showed it to Michael, he fell off the chair. Even the cashier was awestruck and envious of her beauty.

"Is she your girlfriend?" inquired the cashier.

"No, she's my wife."

"You're a lucky man," she remarked.

"I certainly am."

"But she is also fortunate. Did anyone ever tell you how gorgeous you are? You two are a stunning couple. I hope you're aware of this."

"Well, thank you very much, Miss," Michael responded, smiling with delight.

Vanessa took a shower once they arrived home, and applied the cosmetics, lotion, and perfume she had purchased. She accented her clothing with a red flower in her hair. Michael's mouth fell when she stepped out of the room. Vanessa looked more stunning than ever. He stood there, appreciating every detail of her. His heart was so quickly smitten that he forgot he was carrying a tiny box he had bought a long time ago, waiting for the perfect occasion to give it to her. Michael reasoned this was the ideal time.

"Is that for me?" Vanessa asked as she saw what Michael was holding. She kept asking him, but Michael was in a daze. He didn't seem to hear her. It was as if he was in a trance.

"Never mind," Vanessa laughed as she grabbed the little box from Michael's grasp. She was taken aback when she opened it. It contained a simple gold bracelet with the inscription "Forever Yours V&M" on the inside.

"Oh, Michael," she said. She hugged him, full of passion, love, and happiness. She kissed Michael, and he felt like he was in a trance again, and it stole both of their breaths away. The kiss started slowly, but quickly became passionate. Each kiss got more forceful, pushing them further into desire. Vanessa stifled a groan as Michael's hands stroked her cheeks.

"Vanessa," he whispered softly.

"Yes," she replied sweetly.

"I'd like to make love to you right now. Should we stop?"

"Would you like to?"

Before Michael could answer, there was a knock on the door. It was Sophia, ready to go to the luau.

Oh, Sophia. You always have a knack for ruining a wonderful moment, he said in hushed tones. Michael sighed, frustrated. He knew he had missed a once-in-a-lifetime opportunity.

Vanessa heard him. She calmed him with a kiss. "Shh. She'll hear you."

And they both laughed as Sophia looked on.

· · ❦ · ·

MICHAEL THOUGHT IT was time to confess his feelings to Vanessa. While she was in the hospital with Sophia volunteering at their outreach program, he was busy all day preparing for a surprise romantic dinner.

Michael went shopping and purchased two cartons of strawberry-scented candles. It was Vanessa's favorite scent. He then went to a flower shop and bought a dozen roses and lilies. He went to the market and grabbed everything he needed for a delicious and romantic meal.

When Vanessa returned home, it was dark. There was no sign of anyone being home. She didn't see Michael's pickup in the driveway. Michael parked it on the next street on purpose.

Where is he?

Her heart shook as she turned on the lamp and glanced around. It was very quiet. She twisted her head when she thought she heard movement in the bedroom.

"Are you there, Michael?"

No one responded. She made her way down the hallway on her tiptoes, her eyes bright with excitement and astonishment. The floor was littered with scented candles and rose petals. Vanessa noticed a faint light coming from beneath their bedroom door. She took her time opening it. In the background, soft, sensuous music was playing.

A table for two was put up in the bedroom, complete with fresh flowers, a linen tablecloth, and napkins. There was red wine and filet mignon with mushroom-wine sauce, roasted lobster tails, steamed mussels, baked potatoes, and bread. There were oysters and strawberries on the table. When Vanessa saw Michael in his bathrobe, kneeling and clutching a bunch of pink lilies, she smiled.

"Oh, Michael," she said.

"I love you, Vanessa," Michael said as he landed a passionate kiss on her lips.

"You never fail to amaze me, Michael. You are the most romantic person in the world."

Michael grabbed her waist, drew her close, and kissed her. Vanessa felt as though she were on fire. She leaned forward and kissed him tenderly, but passionately. Michael had the sensation that he was floating in mid-air. They hugged, and then he moved his face away, gazed into Vanessa's eyes, and kissed her again.

As Vanessa freshened up, Michael opened the red wine. When she came out with only a towel covering her, he could not control himself anymore. Michael scooped her off her feet as she put her arms around his head, drawing him into a kiss as he carried her to the bed. Michael looked her in the eyes as he removed the towel and dropped it on the floor. Vanessa touched his open lips and felt his warm breath against her fingertips. It filled their gazes with a burning yearning to be one as they came to a standstill and peered into each other's eyes.

And fireworks lit up the night.

·· ~∞~ ··

MICHAEL OPENED HIS eyes with a smile on his face. He could still feel the earth moving from their lovemaking a few hours ago. He shifted his gaze to Vanessa. She was asleep.

"It's time to wake up, my sweet," Michael said, kissing her.

"What time is it?"

"It's four o'clock in the morning."

Vanessa yawned and giggled as she pulled the sheets over herself.

"It's too early," she remarked. "Don't go fishing today. Just stay with me. I love you, Michael," she murmured, looking him in the eyes. "I love you with all my heart, soul, and being." They then had another deep and intense kiss, without taking their hands off each other. They made love again until they were exhausted and fell asleep in each other's arms.

Vanessa's eyes opened as the sun rose, and her lips curved into a gentle smile when she smelled fresh-brewed coffee. She put on the robe and tied the belt around her waist. She was ready to proceed to the kitchen when Michael entered, holding the food tray. Smoke rose from the coffee cup, and fried eggs with toast and orange marmalade were placed on the platter.

"A nice English breakfast for my lovely wife."

"You don't have to do this, Michael. I should have brought you breakfast in bed."

"No, it is our special day. You and I will spend the entire day in bed."

"What exactly do you mean?" she asked teasingly.

"I'd want to do more of what we did last night," Michael jokingly winked at her.

"Naughty boy," Vanessa laughed as Michael slipped back into bed, where they had spent the whole day making love.

For three days, Michael did not go out to sea. His boat was completely dry. His fishing gear and equipment were untouched. The windows and doors remained shut. Michael and Vanessa never tired of rediscovering themselves. They continued to snuggle beneath the cover, relishing the sensation of touching each other's bodies and the steady descent from the night's moments of passion. They were lying face-to-face on their sides, pressed together. As he hugged Vanessa, Michael kissed her on the lips. Vanessa never felt more content, protected, and loved while she smiled and kissed him on the lips. Michael mumbled lovely nothings into her ears, and she muttered something back, giggling and enjoying every second of their time together until they fell asleep.

When Vanessa awoke, Michael had already started roasting hotdogs and skewering marshmallows over an open fire while listening to soft music. There was chilled wine, cheese, crackers, and grapes. Michael didn't mind the unusual pairings.

Vanessa arranged the sleeping bags, pillows, and blankets in the living room. They cuddled in front of the TV and had another magical moment together until the early hours of the morning.

The next morning, Michael was reluctant to get up. It was time for him to set sail. He hadn't gone for a few days. Michael looked over at Vanessa, who was sound asleep. He didn't want to leave, but his buddies were waiting for him at the dock. One thing was clear: Michael planned to propose to Vanessa. He desired a proper marriage for them. He didn't care what happened after. Vanessa was his forever love.

· · ✺ · ·

"ARE YOU INSANE?" DR. Fletcher asked. He'd just returned from a visit to his daughter in Japan.

Michael had just informed the doctor that he intended to marry Vanessa again, and had requested he serve as his best man.

"What happens if she regains her memory? What comes next? I'm pleased you found the woman of your dreams, and if the circumstances were different, I'd be happy for you. She's a sweet girl, but you know deep down that this isn't right. She suffers from memory loss. You're taking advantage of her situation. We might end up in jail for this."

"Doc, what are you talking about?"

"I know you lied to me, Michael. Vanessa isn't your wife. You are not a married man."

Michael was drenched in perspiration. "Doc, how did you find out? Who told you that? And what do you mean, we may end up in jail?"

"Listen, Michael. I was sitting next to an old woman while waiting for my flight from Japan to Honolulu, and we spoke.

She told me about this tiny store in a village and showed me a porcelain geisha girl she bought wrapped in the folds of an old newspaper. It wasn't the figurine that drew my attention. It was an article about a missing heiress who had gone missing at sea. They never found her body, and her parents hoped she was still alive. There was a photo of a beautiful woman wearing makeup and expensive jewelry. The newspaper article was published roughly six months ago. I recognize Vanessa with or without the makeup, fine clothing, and jewelry. I know it's her. What I don't understand is how you knew her name was Vanessa. When you took her to the hospital, she had amnesia. How did you know, Michael?"

As he spoke, Michael's eyes welled up with tears. Dr. Fletcher knew his secret, and he couldn't deny it anymore.

"Doc, please don't tell anyone. I love her, and I will die if I lose her now."

"You know, I care about you, Michael. I've known you since your infancy. Your parents and I were friends since nursery school. I will devote my life to you, but I will not be around for long to support you if something bad happens to you."

"Doc, what do you mean?" He stuttered.

"I'm sorry to tell you I've resigned from my position, Michael. I'm going to move my practice to Japan. My daughter and my new grandchild require my attention. I'm just here for a few days to attend to some personal things before returning to Japan. But don't worry, I'll be back shortly. I told the hospital that I would stay on as head of staff until they found a replacement."

"Doc, I'm going to miss you!"

"I know you'll be OK, Michael. You are stronger than you think, but you must do the right thing."

• • ❦ • •

THE BOAT FINALLY CAME. The people boarded once the bell rang. Dr. Fletcher and Michael exchanged hugs. He was scheduled to fly to Japan today.

"Promise me, you'll tell her everything," Dr. Fletcher said as he boarded the boat. "Don't put it off too long. For Vanessa's sake, you must make this right."

"I promise," he said, waving at him.

Michael was sitting on the beach, unsure of what to do. Dr. Fletcher had long gone, but his mind could still hear his voice. How could he keep his promise when he was in love with Vanessa? Michael didn't want to give up on her just now. He knew well that what he was doing was illegal. At first, it was a game to teach Vanessa some lessons in humility, respect, and compassion. He didn't expect to fall in love with her, or perhaps he did. It perplexed him. He had planned to tell Vanessa everything, but he decided against it. His feelings for her were so strong that they were obscuring his ability to make rational decisions. He was reluctant to risk what they have. He wanted to relish every moment with her for the time being.

Vanessa quickly blended in with the locals. She socialized with the women in the village, and she and Michael soon attended the monthly luau. Vanessa learned how to eat Spam Musubi, a popular snack or meal made of spam, rice, and seaweed. Lomi salmon, poi, Kalua pig, haupia, and other Hawaiian dishes were favorites of hers. Michael had to keep telling Vanessa to take her time chewing her food. Vanessa simply laughed and continued to eat it as if she had tasted nothing like it before. She said she couldn't get enough of it, oblivious to the fact that it was her least favorite cuisine in the world.

Vanessa's small catering business thrived. Her exotic food became well known. Some island visitors would see her and request special orders to take home with them. When these folks returned home, they shared the delicious food with their family and friends. Soon, Vanessa's dish received extraordinary raves on social media without her awareness. With its success, Michael launched a restaurant called "Vanessa's," much to his wife's joy. She prepared the food, while Michael supplied the seafood. When he wasn't out fishing, he helped in the kitchen. Sophia offered to help at first, but Vanessa eventually hired her as a hostess to assist customers at their tables. Sophia enjoyed interacting with individuals who genuinely liked her. Vanessa employed an assistant cook, a server, and a busboy to help with dish washing and table cleaning. They had a fantastic set-up. They laminated the menu on the table so that guests could write their orders on paper and place them on a holder for the server to pick up.

Vanessa's restaurant showed no signs of slowing down.

CHAPTER FOURTEEN

Tom Grandeville attended a board meeting in downtown Los Angeles. It was a productive morning for everyone. Tom was pleased with their future business projects, which included gaining more properties to develop. During a quick break, he spoke with Frederick Davenport, a long-time board member and friend. He was a wealthy businessman who enjoyed traveling with his wife. His daughter, Rachel, was friends with his daughter, Vanessa.

"How was your recent trip, Fred?" he asked.

"It was fantastic. My wife and I had a great time in Honolulu. We discovered this charming little island, and my wife hopes to return there soon. She loved the inhabitants, and the cuisine at this quaint café on the island of Towi was delicious."

"Towi Island? I've never heard of the place."

"Neither do I. Towi is a tiny island near Honolulu. We didn't even know about it until my wife and I went to a charity event in Waikiki. One of the guests mentioned a little eatery named Vanessa's. She spoke highly of it. It intrigued my wife, and she wanted to see it, so we went. It's a cross between a delicious home-cooked meal and exotic food. The aroma was amazing. You and Martha should try it."

"Vanessa's? Towi Island, near Honolulu?" Tom paused, thinking.

We've searched for our daughter throughout the neighboring Hawaiian Islands, but I don't recall exploring an island called Towi.

After Vanessa went missing in the water, he and his wife never stopped looking for her, believing their daughter was still alive. The rescue team and volunteers participated in the search, but after months of unsuccessful searching, all operations were suspended. Tom enlisted the help of a privately trained team to continue the search.

"Towi is a little island. You can't even see it on the map," Fred added.

Tom was overjoyed. Did they miss this island while looking for Vanessa? Was it just a coincidence that there was a restaurant called Vanessa's? He doubted it was his daughter, because she couldn't operate any kitchen appliances, let alone cook. This was likely a wild goose chase, but it was worth a look. Even though it's a minor detail, they should not disregard it. Tom immediately called his wife and told her about the island and the restaurant.

"Do you suppose Vanessa ended up there? Do you think the residents saved her? If that's the case, why hasn't she phoned us, and what's the deal with this restaurant?" Martha asked several times.

"Calm down, Martha. We don't know if it's her, but it's the only lead we have. We need to get there as quickly as possible. Pack our belongings, and I'll have our plane ready."

In less than two hours, Tom and Martha boarded their private jet, ecstatic with the possibility that their daughter was still alive. When they arrived in Honolulu, a limousine took them to their newly built resort, The Grandevilles, in Waikiki. Adam, the hotel manager, greeted them.

"Sir, the helicopter will take off as soon as you are ready."

"Good," Tom said. "Please handle our luggage. We want to leave immediately."

"Yes, sir," he said.

Adam signaled for the bellboy to come forward. He directed him to take the Grandeville's luggage to the chopper, and then he walked up to Tom and Martha and told them to follow him.

"This way, sir, ma'am."

Tom and Martha followed Adam to the helipad. A few moments later, they were flying across the sky. Martha continued holding Tom's hand, eager and nervous. She couldn't wait to land. She was hopeful.

The helicopter landed in a nearby field an hour later. The hotel's driver was waiting for them. Tom's secretary arranged everything.

"Please take us to Vanessa's restaurant as soon as possible!" Tom said to the driver.

"As you wish, sir," the driver said.

"Could you tell me who owns the restaurant?" Tom asked as soon as they entered the car.

"Michael and Vanessa are a well-liked couple on the island. They own Vanessa's restaurant. It's a popular place here in town. Michael was born here. His parents died a few years ago."

"What about Vanessa? Tell us everything you know about her."

"Vanessa is the chef. It was funny, since she couldn't cook when we met her. She appeared fragile, as if she had never worked a day in her life. I think she discovered her inspiration, since she has prepared incredible meals that everyone on the island loves. The first time she hosted the luau, she cooked the best Kalua pig, better than the locals," the driver laughed.

Martha was disappointed when she heard that.

"It couldn't be our daughter, Tom. Vanessa despises luaus and the sight of a roasted pig."

"You're right. It can't be Vanessa," Tom responded dejectedly. "Since we're already here, we might as well enjoy it. Let's check if Fred is speaking the truth when he brags about that eatery."

Martha let out a disappointed groan.

"Don't worry, Martha. We will not give up. We will find our daughter."

The vehicle came to a stop in front of Vanessa's restaurant moments later.

"Please call me when you're ready to leave," the driver remarked.

Tom nodded.

"Hey Michael, I brought your customers from the mainland," the driver said, smiling.

Michael turned around and waved to the driver, before greeting Tom and Martha.

"Welcome to Vanessa's. Is this your first time here? I am sure you will enjoy our food."

Both Tom and Martha nodded. Michael found them a table in the corner.

"Is this all right?"

"Yes, this is fine," Tom said.

Michael showed them the laminated menu on the table and informed them that the special of the day was chicken with coconut milk. He told them he'd be right back to take their order.

"The menu items seem excellent, Tom," Martha said. "According to our driver, Vanessa is the chef here. She is definitely not our daughter. Vanessa does not know how to turn on a stove or boil water."

"Shh, let's order. I'm starving. We'll think about it better once we've eaten."

Martha chose shrimp and chicken pasta, while Tom ordered shrimp and crab Louie. He also ordered the day's special chicken with coconut milk and an exotic non-alcoholic drink.

A few minutes later, Michael reappeared with their drinks. After that, he returned with their meal. Martha took a bite. The food was delicious. Even Tom, who was a finicky eater, appreciated his salad and chicken.

"This is incredible. The chef threw something unusual in here that tastes fantastic," said Tom.

Martha sampled Tom's chicken with coconut milk, and the shrimp and crab Louie. Tom tried Martha's shrimp and chicken pasta. They were divine.

Martha glanced around and saw Michael serving another guest. She waved for him to come over.

"My compliments to the chef. This was the best lunch I'd ever had. Can we meet the chef and thank her?"

"Of course. We're busy right now. It'll take a few minutes if you don't mind waiting."

"Don't worry, we haven't finished yet. I'd want to try your desserts," Martha stated.

Martha and Tom enjoyed their pineapple flan. It was another fantastic dish from the chef. They both agreed it was the tastiest lunch they'd had in a long time.

"This chef will make a name for herself. She prepares the most amazing meals, and everything appears one-of-a-kind," Martha added, and Tom agreed.

It was a busy day at the restaurant. Michael continued returning, telling Tom and Martha that he hadn't forgotten about them. Martha replied it was fine for them to wait.

"What a charming young man," Martha said.

"You're correct. I've noticed everyone on this island is friendly," Tom added. "I don't mind staying longer to explore this place."

"Me, too," Martha concurred. "How about you pay for our meal and we check in at the hotel so we can start exploring?"

"What about the chef? Didn't you say you wanted to meet her?"

"We'll see her later when we return for supper."

. . ⚬⚬ . .

"SWEETHEART, STOP FOR a moment to greet these people. They wanted to compliment you. They've been waiting a long time, and I feel terrible that I have to apologize all the time," Michael explained.

"All right, let me place this order on the plate. Go on, and I'll meet you outside."

Michael nodded and went away.

Vanessa cleaned her face and examined herself in a little mirror on the wall. She came out of the kitchen, looking for

Michael. She saw him conversing with two distinguished individuals.

As she walked toward them, Tom saw her. He blinked numerous times because he feared his eyes were playing tricks on him. He grasped Martha's hand, and when she turned around and saw her daughter, she burst out crying. She couldn't believe it. Vanessa was alive and well.

"Hello, my name is Vanessa. I'm the chef here. Michael told me you liked the food. That pleases me. Thank you very much."

Martha and Tom sobbed.

"Ma'am, are you okay?" Vanessa asked, concerned.

"Vanessa, my dear daughter," Martha said as she wrapped her arms around her. Tom chimed in.

"Sweetheart, we looked everywhere for you. We were so worried. Why didn't you call us?" asked Tom.

It took Vanessa by surprise. She did not know why these people were acting this way. What were they saying?

"I'm sorry. Do I know you?" Vanessa asked.

Tom and Martha exchanged puzzled looks. Why didn't their daughter recognize them?

Michael was gripped in dread as he realized what was unfolding in front of him. He was horrified, as if he had seen a ghost. Even though he knew it was going to happen eventually, it still sent shivers down Michael's spine. Vanessa's parents had found her, something he had feared for a long time. His heart pounded as his worry reached uncontrollable levels. He knew he'd lost her, and the thought of being apart from her horrified him. Michael could feel his heart separating. He should've told Vanessa the truth sooner. He should have heeded Dr. Fletcher's advice. He warned him, but now it was too late.

"Vanessa, you don't remember us? We are your parents. You're our missing daughter who went missing at sea some months ago," Martha wailed, perplexed.

"You must be mistaken. My name is Vanessa Angelo," she said, staring at her. "Come to think of it, the doctor who examined me, Dr. Fletcher, informed me I had been in an accident at sea and lost my memory, but that my husband had saved me."

"Husband? Are you married?" Martha asked.

Vanessa grabbed Michael's hand and introduced him. Michael found it difficult to look at Martha and Tom. He continued averting his gaze from Vanessa.

"Are you okay, sweetheart? You seem distracted," Vanessa asked. "Do you believe they're telling the truth? Their story about my being their daughter and me being lost at sea seemed to fit."

Michael remained silent.

"We are your parents, sweetheart. We've been searching for you for a long time. You and your friends had a boating accident in Honolulu. You were there to celebrate your twenty-first birthday. We were told you went sailing, but there was a terrible storm, and you were lost at sea. The Coastguard saved your friends, but you were not with them. We looked everywhere for you. They featured you in newspapers, radios, TVs, and even on the internet. You have been missing for nearly a year. But we never gave up hope that one day we would find you," Martha said, her eyes welling up with emotions.

Michael's eyes, too, were blurred by tears. He trembled in front of Vanessa. He tried to speak, but couldn't find his voice.

"A year ago? Lost at sea? I realize the events were similar, but there has to be a reason for this. I'm sure it's purely coincidental. Please tell them, Michael. I'm freaking out here!" Vanessa asked as she took a step back to look at him, her gaze scouring his face for answers.

Still, Michael remained silent. He couldn't speak because he was gripped with emotion. Vanessa was perplexed as she looked at him. Something didn't seem right. She couldn't figure out why Michael looked terrified and had tears in his eyes, as if he was crying. She cast a suspicious glance at him.

"Please, Vanessa, don't look at me like that," Michael pleaded.

"What are you talking about, Michael? I don't understand."

"Don't forget how much I love you, Vanessa. I am sorry for deceiving you."

Vanessa had the impression that something was awry. What was Michael's reason for apologizing? Was she correct in her assumption that Michael had been harboring secrets from her the whole time?

Michael grasped her hand, but she pushed it away.

"Don't! Please, Michael, just tell me the truth. Do you know what's going on?" she urged.

Michael's eyes welled up with tears, which he brushed away with his sleeves. He swallowed before speaking.

"Vanessa, you and I were never married. We didn't even date. I recognized you right away when I found you drifting into the ocean and drew you in. We met a few times in Honolulu before your accident, but you don't remember it. Don't you see? It was fate. I didn't intend for this to happen. Please believe me when I tell you how much I love you," Michael stated. He kissed and embraced her as though he didn't want to let her go.

Vanessa covered her face, her mind whirling. Something near her heart clenched.

"No!" she cried, shaking her head as if to clear her mind of what she had heard. Her rage was exploding. "Michael, if you're kidding, this is a poor joke."

"I'm afraid it's true," he said. "I'm sorry."

"And you've been silent all this time? Why didn't you tell me? But now I see how you kept up the deception, how you've been stringing me along for months."

"Stringing you along? Is that what you thought I'd been doing? I know you know me better than that, Vanessa," he murmured, tears welling up again. "I'm sorry for misleading you. I'd wanted to tell you for a long time, but I didn't want to hurt you. I was waiting for the right moment, but I was also afraid of losing you, and the thought horrified me. I can't live without you," he whispered, his voice quivering. "Vanessa, please. I love you so much."

Vanessa's eyes welled up with tears as she responded. "You have no idea how much this hurts."

Michael's heart was pounding. He could feel his world collapsing around him.

"Oh, God, I trusted you," Vanessa sobbed again.

She turned to see everyone in the restaurant staring at them. She could see their stunned and terrified expressions. As Vanessa saw her life crumble around her, her head spun, and the room darkened. She fell and hit her head on the table. Her mother screamed when she saw blood flowing down her daughter's face.

"Vanessa!"

CHAPTER FIFTEEN

Vanessa opened her eyes and focused her attention on the figure in front of her. A soft voice murmured in her ear. It was Dr. Fletcher. He'd only just arrived on Towi Island when he heard about Vanessa's mishap. He dashed to the hospital to check on her condition.

"Hello, Vanessa. I'm Dr. Fletcher. Last night, they brought you to the hospital. You had a severe head injury, but an MRI revealed everything looked normal. The helicopter will arrive soon to transport you to Honolulu. Michael loves you. I want you to know that. I saw him earlier, and he wants me to tell you he will always love you. Michael attempted to see you, but your parents prevented it. He said he'd wait for you until you returned home."

"Michael?" Vanessa muttered before collapsing.

· · ⚮ · ·

VANESSA STRUGGLED TO open her eyes. She looked around and realized she was in an unfamiliar place. A ceiling fan agitated the air with a whispering sound from the blades, and adjustable lights lit the room.

"Where am I?"

"You are in a private room at a hospital in Honolulu. You had a concussion. How are you, honey?" asked Martha.

"M-mom! Is that you?"

"Did you say, Mom? Vanessa, do you know who I am? Do you remember what happened to you?"

"I believe so. I'm trying to piece everything together, but my head hurts."

"You took a direct hit to the head. It appears to have healed your amnesia. Just take it slowly. You should get some rest. I'll call the doctor."

"Mom?"

"Yes, dear."

"Where is Michael? I want to see him."

"Michael planned this whole thing. You didn't know who the man was. He recognized you, but he did not notify the authorities. We spent a long time searching for you, but he never came forward to tell us you were living with him. He took advantage of you because he knew you had amnesia," Martha explained.

Vanessa cried. She loved Michael. Even after all her mother had said, she still wanted to be with him.

"I need to see Michael, Mom. Where is he? He promised he would never leave me."

"Ness, sweetie. Michael betrayed you. After what transpired at the restaurant, we never saw him again," her mother claimed. She reasoned that it would be better if her daughter believed Michael had abandoned her. But it was more difficult than she expected.

"Michael would never do something like that. He is crazy about me. I need to see him," Vanessa said.

"Listen, honey. Michael took advantage of your situation. Look at your hands. They're harsh and overworked. You were his slave."

"No, Mom. Michael treated me like a princess. He adores me, and I love him."

"Listen, Vanessa. We intend to press charges against him. He'll be imprisoned. Do you understand? He'll pay for what he did to you."

It took Vanessa by surprise. She kept shaking her head.

"You can't do that."

"Of course, we can. He must be held accountable for what he did to you. Do you have any idea how many lives he ruined? Your father and I, as well as your brothers, spent months looking for you. We spent nearly a year sailing around Honolulu and other islands, hoping to find you. And how about you? You slaved away many days and nights working for that man. We'll make sure he's locked up for a long time."

"No, Mom, I don't want Michael to go to prison. I will go peacefully with you. Just drop the charges, and I will never see him again," said Vanessa as she wept.

Martha took her daughter into her arms to comfort her. She had never seen Vanessa cry over a man before.

She must truly love him, but in time, she would learn to forget him. I'll make sure of that, her mother thought.

Vanessa stayed at the hospital for another day before flying back to Los Angeles. She waited for Michael to see her, but he never came to visit her.

Maybe my parents were right. Michael only used me, she mumbled to herself, tears streaming down her cheeks.

The overcast sky provided an appropriate background for Vanessa as she made her way to their private jet to Los Angeles. As they boarded the plane, Martha noticed the emptiness in her daughter's eyes. She gave Tom a sidelong glance, but he ignored her.

Vanessa had remained silent during the flight, staring out the window. When they landed at a private airport in Los Angeles, she was unhappy. Vanessa couldn't help but miss Michael. She loved him more than she'd ever loved anyone.

·· ✎ ··

THERE WAS A BANNER that said, "Welcome home, Vanessa!" hanging over the gate to the elite residential area. Outside, photographers and reporters waited for an interview. They were curious to know what had happened to Vanessa during the months she was missing. To keep the driveway clear, Tom alerted security personnel, who shooed everyone away. When the gate opened, the driver didn't slow down, and the limousine sped through the gate.

Vanessa walked into the house and saw her friends Rachel, Jennifer, Samantha, Stephanie, and Alexandra seated in the living room, delighted to see her. Vanessa couldn't get herself excited, no matter how hard she tried.

"I don't want to see my friends right now, Mom. Could you just tell them to come back another time?"

"Sure, Ness, whatever you want. I'll take you to your room and leave you to relax. I'll take care of everything."

Vanessa nodded as they made their way to her room. Her mother kissed her on the cheeks as she sat on the side of the bed. Vanessa sobbed in bed for a long time when she was alone. She yearned for Michael.

Why didn't he drop by the hospital to see me? Why didn't he show his face after what he'd done? She wept bitter tears, and it took her a long time to fall asleep.

Vanessa, tired of crying, joined her parents and brothers for supper that night. Everyone remained silent. Vanessa broke into tears unexpectedly, which startled everyone.

"Are you okay?" Jason was worried.

Vanessa said nothing.

"I know you are heartbroken, but in time, I am sure you will forget his name."

Vanessa took a deep breath and let it out.

"His name is Michael, and I'm certain I'll never forget him."

"You know, you can't keep doing this. It upset everyone. Why don't you explain things to me, and I'll try my best to follow along?"

"Do you think I'm going to tell you? You're working against me. Nothing in this house is important anymore."

"That is unfair, Vanessa. You know how much we love you. We're simply concerned with your well-being," Martha explained.

"Vanessa, sweetheart, you've been crying and going without food for the last few hours since we left Honolulu. You have had nothing to eat. Please eat," her father begged.

Vanessa was not in the mood to argue.

"I will not discuss it tonight," she said, her voice irritated. "I'm going to bed."

Vanessa stayed in her room the next day, not going downstairs for breakfast or lunch. Vanessa refused to eat when the maid brought food to her room, and the maid became worried. She informed Vanessa's mother.

Martha walked upstairs and repeatedly knocked on Vanessa's door, but there was no answer. Martha tried again, and when she received no response and the door remained shut, she knew something was wrong. She took the master key from the drawer and unlocked the door to find Vanessa weeping; her face hidden under the pillow.

"Vanessa, are you all right, sweetheart?"

"Mom!" exclaimed Vanessa as she sprang out of bed and into her arms.

"He lied to me, Mom! I've never been so angry or felt so outraged. I hate him, and yet sometimes I feel I need him more than ever. I loved him with all my heart. Why would he do such a thing after I had given him everything?" Vanessa stated as she lowered her head.

Martha got the distinct impression that something had occurred between Vanessa and Michael. After all, they were addressed on the island as husband and wife, but she refused to believe it. She was hyperventilating as she clutched her chest and struggled to breathe. Martha vented her rage as tears streamed down her cheeks after she had relaxed and calmed herself.

"I'm sorry for disappointing you, Mom."

"Disappointed with you? Never! Am I enraged? Yes, but not directed at you. I'm angry because Michael took advantage of your condition."

"I'm sorry, Mom."

Martha smiled at her daughter.

"Shh... We will fix this. Don't worry. The first thing you should do is eat. Then I'd like you to rest."

"Yes, mother."

Martha glanced sympathetically at her daughter. She shut the door behind her and went downstairs to the kitchen to get some dinner for her.

. . ⚶ . .

MICHAEL SAT ON THE trunk of a coconut tree that had fallen on the beach during a hurricane month earlier. It was his favorite place to go when he needed some alone time to think. His thoughts raced in a thousand directions. He was carrying a bottle of hard liquor, attempting to drown his sorrows.

"Vanessa! I'm sorry for hurting you. Please forgive me. I was wrong, and I can't live without you. Please come back."

Michael still could not accept that the love of his life was gone. He was furious beyond belief, and he couldn't accept he would never see Vanessa again. It seems like only yesterday they were happy together, kissing, cuddling, and making love.

Why does it have to end this way?

As his emotions emerged, he had flashbacks of what had transpired. When Vanessa passed out in the restaurant, Michael rushed to the hospital's emergency room. While he was in the waiting area, Vanessa's father told him to stay away from his daughter. Michael lingered in the lobby, but was immediately escorted out by security guards. He pleaded with them to allow him to speak with Vanessa's parents at least, but security was under strict orders not to let him in. Michael contacted Dr. Fletcher and requested he check on Vanessa's condition. Michael sat in his truck in the parking lot waiting to hear from the doctor, but security approached him and ordered him to leave the area.

Michael left the hospital, but returned a few hours later. He had not slept at all. He stepped right through the main entrance, but security personnel stopped him and denied him entry.

"We're sorry, Michael, but we have strict orders not to allow you into the hospital."

"Kevin, this is absurd. You know me. Please allow me to see Vanessa. She needs me," Michael begged.

"I'm sorry, Michael. I want to help you, but I'm just doing my job."

Michael needed to see Vanessa. He was back in the parking lot, pacing the ground to the point where he thought he was going crazy. He waited in his truck, hoping to see her, but there was no information on her whereabouts. It concerned him. Michael needed to speak with Dr. Fletcher. He didn't know if the doctor had conveyed his message to Vanessa. He tried calling the doctor, but could not do so.

Michael had been scouting the hospital for several hours. Having not seen Vanessa, his intense rage had piled up into a boiling point of feeling about to burst. He parked his truck behind the building, near Dr. Fletcher's automobile, hoping he'd see him. Michael sat in his vehicle, and he must have dozed off because of weariness when he heard a repeated tapping noise over his head. He opened his eyes, surprised to see Dr. Fletcher with the saddest eyes he had ever seen. He'd had the worst shock of his life when the doctor told him Vanessa and her family had left on a chopper bound for Honolulu a few hours ago.

"I delivered your message to Vanessa as they brought her into the ICU, but she was in and out of consciousness. I'm not sure if she heard me. Sorry, Michael. I should have told you sooner, but I lost my phone on the plane. I only hoped you'd remember that I always parked my car behind the building. It was such a relief to see you from the window above."

Michael couldn't believe it. He squandered time, waiting for nothing.

"Doc, do you know where they took Vanessa?"

Dr. Fletcher could sense the loss, sorrow, and grief in Michael's eyes.

"I'm sorry, Michael. They didn't tell us anything. They shrouded everything in secrecy. Vanessa's parents made certain no one knew where they took her."

Michael felt his world crumble around him. He gritted his teeth and screamed at the top of his lungs. He was terrified of the possibilities. Michael was concerned he might never see Vanessa again. He couldn't breathe. He felt as though a thousand needles were taking turns stabbing at his heart. His existence was worthless without Vanessa.

Michael couldn't recall how he got home. He had no idea how long he had been sitting on the balcony, catatonic and zombie-like, never shifting or moving from his chair. He didn't care and thought his life was leaving him until he heard a calming sound, the voice of a woman.

"Don't give up, Michael. Vanessa loves you more than life itself. You must be strong. You must track her down and fight for her."

Michael kept hearing Sophia's voice in his head. She stood behind him, watching him. Sophia's voice was faint for an old woman, and Michael could barely hear her, yet it was powerful enough to shake him out of his daze.

"Thank you, Sophia," Michael said as he hugged the elderly woman. "You're right; I have to fight for the woman I love."

Sophia smiled and appeared glad to see Michael restore his desire to live. Michael lost no time in contacting his friend Daniel in Honolulu to arrange for a helicopter to pick him up.

Two hours later, Michael was on his way to find Vanessa. He couldn't sit still, since he was so excited to see her. When Michael arrived, Daniel was waiting for him, giving him a list of hospitals in Honolulu and tossing him his car keys, which Michael grabbed in one swoop. He dashed to his car and sped across town amid rush hour traffic. Michael checked the hospitals on the list and drove from one to the next, asking the same questions and getting the same answer: Vanessa was not a patient. And the more he thought about it, the more it pointed to one thing. He'd never see Vanessa again.

It had been a long day. Michael was becoming frustrated and had given up hope of ever seeing Vanessa again. He walked like a zombie to the parking lot. It was the last hospital on the list, and they informed him that there was no Vanessa Grandeville patient there. He grew furious, bewildered, and on the edge of a panic attack.

As he turned to leave, he looked back at the hospital's main door and was shocked to see Vanessa in a wheelchair being pushed to a limousine. Michael rushed toward her, but the limo had already driven away. He dashed back to his car and followed them. Michael felt discouraged when he saw the limousine turn into a private airport. He tried to enter, but the security guard refused to let him in without a pass.

"Vanessa!" Michael screamed his lungs out. "I love you, Vanessa!" Michael sobbed on the ground. He grieved and sighed as the plane took off. Michael knew he'd never see Vanessa again. With a sad heart, he returned to his car, checked himself into a cheap motel, and proceeded to a local pub to drown his sorrows.

Instead of checking out the next day, Michael stayed at the motel and returned to the same pub to drink more. He was at a loss for words. Vanessa was his entire world. He couldn't take it any longer and sobbed alone in his room. Michael wept so loudly that passersby on the street could hear him. He disturbed the other hotel guests, causing the manager to kick him out.

Michael decided it was time to go home and board the ferry back to Towi Island. When he arrived, he was surprised to see two men in black suits waiting for him. Michael attempted to instigate a fight with them when they handed him a Temporary Protective Order to keep away from Vanessa, but the two guys shoved him down to the ground. They added that if he violated the order for any reason, Mr. Grandeville would charge him with abduction and imprison him for a long time. The two men departed and hopped into a helicopter to take off.

Michael stood in front of Vanessa's and could not believe in the blink of an eye that Vanessa was gone. He walked inside the restaurant and sat alone in the dark, empty room. Suddenly, Michael heard a disturbance in the kitchen and ran to investigate. He thought he had heard Vanessa call him. He hesitated for a while to be sure it wasn't his mind playing tricks on him, but there it was again.

"I knew you'd come back, Vanessa. I knew you'd find your way back to me," Michael said, but when he entered the kitchen, no one was there. It was all a figment of his imagination.

Michael snapped back to the present. The thought of life without Vanessa made him feel helpless. The only thing that mattered to him was her.

"Vanessa, Vanessa!" he screamed, repeatedly crying out her name. He felt a sudden shortness of breath. "Why did you leave me? Vanessa, I love you!"

· · ∽⚬∾ · ·

A WEEK HAD PASSED SINCE Michael returned home. Raul and his buddies were concerned when they didn't see him. Even the restaurant stayed closed. Sophia thought something terrible had happened to Michael. With her persistence, the local police showed up at Michael's house. They located an opening and entered. He wasn't at home. The police then proceeded to Vanessa's restaurant and knocked on the door, but there was no answer. They entered through an unlocked rear door and found Michael lying on the floor, unconscious. They rushed him to the hospital, where Dr. Fletcher examined him.

"What's wrong with you, Michael?" Dr. Fletcher asked. But Michael remained silent and stared out the window.

"I understand how painful it is to be dumped by someone you love, but you knew from the start that the life you established with her wasn't real," the doctor explained. "You knew she had amnesia, but you created this world with her. She had to return to her family. That was the right thing to do."

"I love her so much, Doc," Michael remarked, with a sorrowful grin. "I need her in my life. I need to find her."

"And then what? Her parents took her away from you. What can you do? The Grandevilles are influential people. Do you even have a plan?"

Michael gazed out the window. The doctor was right. He couldn't justify what he'd done. He couldn't wrap his head around it. Michael required a strategy to convince Vanessa to return home.

"Michael, you built a relationship with Vanessa, the one with the memory loss. That Vanessa is long gone. She will remain a memory. Be thankful you shared your life with her, even if it was for a short time. It is better to fall in love than never to have loved at all."

Michael remained silent and continued to gaze out the window. He couldn't live without Vanessa. That was clear to him. Michael missed her more than he could have imagined. He couldn't stop thinking about her every minute of every hour of the day.

Dr. Fletcher released Michael a few days later, but not before giving him another pep talk and telling him to be strong.

"Life is always a struggle. Make a plan before you act. The most important thing to remember is not to neglect your health. What if Vanessa came home and saw you like that, all skin and bones? One look at you, and she'll fly back to where she came from."

Michael's face lit up with a little smile as he heard it. He grinned and thanked the doctor. Dr. Fletcher was basically telling him to go after Vanessa. The concept was not impossible. All he needed was time to calm down and collect his thoughts.

CHAPTER SIXTEEN

Michael went to the library and searched for the Grandeville family on the internet. He hoped to learn more about them and where they lived. Unfortunately, the addresses were only directed at companies in Los Angeles.

Well, that's a lead worth following up on, he reasoned.

Michael wasted little time getting his boat ready to sail back to Honolulu. He sailed for a few hours. As he drew closer to the shore, he shut off the motor and floated the last few feet, before tying up his boat to the dock. Michael was walking to the travel agency with a light travel bag when he saw two guys following him. They weren't the same two men who had served him with a protection order. He was certain it wasn't a coincidence that the men seemed to walk in the same direction as he did.

Michael entered an MDLM store, picked up a magazine, and flipped through it. He monitored the door to see whether the men would follow him there. Sure enough, two guys in black suits walked in, and Michael watched them scan the store. As the men moved toward the back, Michael sneaked up to the front door and opened it on tiptoe. His heart was pounding in his chest. He made his way down the road, occasionally looking back to make sure no one followed him. Michael walked two blocks in a circle. He returned to the travel agency, thinking he had lost the men. To his surprise, the two men were waiting for him on the curb. He did not know where he was heading. He was running out of time. Michael grinned as he realized Ernesto's Club was just around the corner. He walked in.

"Michael, you returned!" Ernesto greeted him as soon as he saw him. They welcomed each other by shaking hands and smiling.

"Ernesto, I require a significant favor. There are two men outside your club, and I know they are following me. They don't want me to go to Los Angeles to see my wife. Do you think you can assist me in distracting them?"

Ernesto frowned, perplexed. He wasn't oblivious, but something visceral kept him from grasping Michael's statements.

"What do you mean?"

Michael remained silent for a minute, unsure of how to answer. Finally, he said, "I screwed up big time, Ernesto."

Ernesto's eyes widened in disbelief as Michael recounted the events that took place when he learned who Vanessa was.

"Did you say Vanessa Florence Grandeville? Is she Tom Grandeville's daughter? The multi-millionaire real estate developer?"

Michael remained silent, but nodded.

"Wow! I've only heard stuff like that in movies. I never imagined it would happen in real life. But I'm up for it. What do you want me to do?" he asked.

"Can you go to a travel agency and get me a ticket on the first available flight to Los Angeles? Do you think you could do that for me?"

Ernesto's face lit up with a broad grin.

"I can do better than that. My girlfriend works as a travel agent. We don't have to go anywhere. She'll handle everything online, and all we have to do is print the ticket here. It's known as an e-ticket. Don't you love new technology? I need to call her and give her the information. It will only take a few minutes to get your ticket."

"That's fantastic!" said Michael as he handed Ernesto his information.

Ernesto left and entered the back room. He returned a few minutes later and said everything was OK.

"You have less than two hours to get to the airport before your plane departs. Don't worry about the ticket. I paid for it."

Ernesto provided him with a copy of his printed ticket to show to the agent at the airport ticket counter.

"Are you sure, Ernesto? Money is not a problem. Let me pay you back."

"Just get your wife back, and when you do, come here and see me, OK? I'd want to meet your wife."

"Of course. Thank you, Ernesto."

Michael peeked out the window to check if the two men in black suits were still outside. They were. Michael and Ernesto devised a scheme to trick them. A few minutes later, Michael exited the bar, intoxicated. He swayed and stumbled to his feet. He tripped and fell. Then Michael stood up and attempted many times, but each time he fell to the ground.

"Oh, that poor guy. He is still broken-hearted. Look at him stumbling on the pavement," observed the first man in a suit, unaware that Michael was missing his travel bag.

"Yeah, nothing to report here," the second man in a suit responded.

"Do we still need to follow him?"

"No, let's not bother that poor man. He's not going anywhere tonight. His boat is on the dock. We'll come back early in the morning. He'll eventually wind up sleeping in the gutter. Let's head home. My wife's birthday is today, and I still have time to get her a lovely present."

The men climbed into their car and drove away. Ernesto watched them leave and rushed to the door, where he saw Michael still playing drunk.

"Michael!" he yelled at him.

When Michael looked back, he saw Ernesto waving at him. "They're gone!"

"Great! Just one more step, and I'd have stumbled for real," Michael joked.

Ernesto drove fast across Honolulu to get to the airport, as they were running late. Michael was fortunate that they arrived in time to say their goodbyes.

"Listen, if you need anything while you're in Los Angeles, here's my brother's number," Ernesto continued as he handed Michael a business card. "Tell him I sent you. He will definitely assist you."

"Thank you, Ernesto. I appreciate all you've done for me. You are a good friend."

"I'm happy to help you, Michael. You helped me before, so now it's my turn to support you. Best wishes, my braddah!"

The two guys hugged until it was time to board the plane for Los Angeles.

• • ⚘ • •

THE PLANE TOUCHED DOWN, and the passengers exited. Michael had no idea where to go. He was seeing Los Angeles for the first time. Michael knew he had to go to Beverly Hills. He couldn't find the Grandeville's exact address, but he read in a magazine that the wealthy and famous frequented it. That's where he intended to begin his quest. He was hoping to strike gold and gather information there. He instructed the cab driver to take him to the nearest Beverly Hills hotel, where the affluent and famous congregate. The taxi driver drove him to the Beverly Hills Mega Resort.

The hotel staff immediately recognized him as a visitor from Hawaii because of the attire he wore: an aloha shirt, jeans, and slippers. Michael was so excited and nervous that he didn't give any thought to what he was going to wear. For him, it's all about getting Vanessa home.

Michael was concerned about staying at the opulent resort. He felt like an outsider, not to mention that it was excessively pricey. This trip cost him all his life's savings, but he didn't care. He did not know what to expect when he arrived at the luxury resort. To his surprise, everyone made him feel welcome from the time he arrived. As soon as he was comfortable in his room, he began to work. He walked to the bar and ordered a drink. Michael nodded to the bartender, an unspoken order for another of the same.

Michael could make everyone feel as though they'd known him their entire lives. He possessed an infectious charm that drew people in and made them want to like him. If Michael tried, within minutes of chatting to him, everybody would swap life stories with him as if they had been best friends their whole lives. He tried to find out from the bartender and the guests if they had any knowledge of the Grandevilles. Unfortunately, he received contradictory information.

Michael charmed Mario, the cleaning supervisor. The first time he saw Mario, he was on the second floor, where he was staying. Mario checked the work of a housekeeper to see whether it was up to par.

Mario and Michael passed each other many times in the hallway. Michael flashed him a sincere smile that almost reached his eyes. Mario felt he was nice. He bowed and grinned back at him, saying, "Good morning, sir."

Michael regarded Mario as friendly and personable immediately. He came to a halt in front of him and struck up a conversation. He asked if he could recommend a destination to see prominent individuals. Mario advised going to Rodeo Drive. He made additional recommendations, and after a few minutes of conversing, Mario felt as if he had known Michael forever. They exchanged stories about their families and where they came from, which helped create a sense of familiarity and trust. They settled into a casual discussion.

"I have a sibling who lives in Honolulu. I haven't seen him in a while, but I hope to pay him a visit one of these days," Mario remarked.

"Yeah, come and visit. Hawaii is a wonderful location to unwind."

"My brother had been nagging me for years to help him with his business. He's a big-time club owner there. Maybe you've heard of it? Ernesto's?"

"Ernesto's?" Michael asked. "Don't tell me Ernesto's Club in Paradise Tower? Are you his younger brother, Mario?"

"That's my brother. How did you come to know him?"

Michael couldn't believe his luck. "What a small world. This is wonderful." He pulled out his phone and called Ernesto's private number. "Hello Ernesto. Yes, I am in Beverly Hills. Yeah, I'm OK, but there's someone here who wants to talk to you."

Michael gave Mario the phone.

"Brother! How are you? Yes. I'm here with Michael. Okay, yeah, okay. I miss you as well, my brother. Yes. I'll see you soon."

Mario handed the phone back to Michael.

"I can't believe it. This is fate, you know," said Mario. "Hey Michael, my brother asked me to help you. I'm not sure what's going on, but I'm sure you'll let me know. My shift finishes in twenty minutes. If you can wait, we'll talk later, OK? I'll show you around town."

"Many thanks, Mario. I hope this isn't too much of a hassle."

"No, I don't mind. I have nothing to do at home today. Just meet me in the lobby in twenty minutes."

. . ⚜ . .

MICHAEL AND MARIO WERE driving down Hollywood Boulevard in a classic black 1982 Porsche 911SC. Mario claimed it was his father's most prized property. When he passed away a few years ago, he left it to him.

"The intersection of Hollywood Boulevard and Highland Avenue is a landmark. We may see the hands and footprints of legendary cinematic actors on the cement courtyard in front of Grauman's Chinese Theater. If you like that, there's the Hollywood Walk of Fame inlaid in the sidewalk and a few museums to visit. There's the Hollywood Bowl and a celebrity and movie star home tour."

"Wait! Did you say celebrity and movie star home tours?"

"Yes, I did."

"What is it?" Michael inquired, excited.

"If you want to see your favorite movie star's house or any prominent person, there's a tour bus for that. It's a two- or three-hour tour. The trip stops at Rodeo Drive, the Hollywood Bowl, Beverly Hills, and other locations. You won't see any celebrities or famous people, believe me, but you will see where they live."

"Beverly Hills? Rodeo Drive? Hollywood? I believe the Grandeville's live nearby."

"Grandeville? Are you referring to Grandeville Properties?"

"Yes, have you heard of them? I'm looking for my wife."

"Your wife is a Grandeville?"

"Yes, but her parents don't approve, so they took her away from me. That is why I am here. I'm looking for her. If she doesn't love me anymore, I need to hear it from her. Otherwise, I'll have to keep hoping and trying to find her."

"Yes, I've heard of Grandeville. They usually stay at the Beverly Hills Mega Resort when they attend an event. The Grandeville's own half of the land around here. They have businesses all over the country."

Michael's mouth dropped open in disbelief, shocked, to be honest. "Are they rich and powerful?" he asked.

"Yes. You didn't know?"

"Vanessa was a spoiled princess, and I knew well that she hailed from an affluent family. I had no idea how powerful and influential they were. I think I just didn't believe it."

Michael was suddenly depressed. He remembered Ernesto telling him the Grandeville's were multi-millionaires. He was so excited and eager to see Vanessa that he wasn't paying attention to what Ernesto was saying.

"There's no way I could compete with that. There's nothing I could give Vanessa that she doesn't already have."

Mario, feeling sad for his new friend, asked, "You love her, don't you?"

"Yes, Mario. I love her more than life itself."

"One thing I've learned in life is that love conquers all. If you love her, you can deal with whatever comes. You can get through it with the strength of your love."

"You're correct, Mario. Vanessa is worth fighting for. I don't care what happens. I will pursue her until I hear from her that she no longer loves me."

"That's my man."

Mario parked his car on the curb.

"Why did you stop?"

Mario signaled for Michael to be quiet while dialing, and spoke in a different tone to the person on the other end.

"Hello Alberto. This is Mario. I'm good. Yeah, I realize it's been a while. Listen, do you still work on the celebrity home tour? Oh, you do. What? You got a promotion? You're a full-time tour driver? That's even better, man! Do you pick up passengers at the Beverly Hills Mega Resort? Great. Get me two tickets, OK? My companion and I will attend your trip tomorrow. Yes, tomorrow. What time? Ten o'clock? We'll see you then. Thanks, Dude!"

"That's my cousin, Alberto," Mario said after hanging up the phone. "We grew up together. So, did you hear? Get ready. We have a date tomorrow at 10 a.m."

Michael thanked Mario with a big smile and a gentle tap on the shoulder. He was only a day away from seeing his lovely wife.

Mario responded with a grin. "You're welcome. Just don't forget to tell Ernesto about it, OK?"

"No worries, Mario. You and your brother helped me so much, and I can't thank you enough."

"It's time to unwind. Now, get me a drink," Mario said.

"You got it!" Michael laughed.

CHAPTER SEVENTEEN

Vanessa's memories were restored with the help of a psychologist. She still had bad days, but everything she remembered was a victory. Vanessa had questioned her parents about what occurred when they transported her from Towi Island to the hospital in Honolulu. Where was Michael all that time? She had to know. She had to ask them. Her recollection was still blurry, and she needed to fill in the blanks. However, her parents provided little information, and she concluded they were concealing the truth from her. Instead, they told her what had happened when they received the dreadful news that her boat had sunk and she had perished.

"We were in London when Jason called and informed us what had happened to you," Martha said. "We traveled directly back to the United States. Your father organized search and rescue teams. They scoured the area with the Coast Guard, police, and volunteers, and it took many days to find your friends. They were saved while they lost you at sea. We didn't know how you got separated from them or wound up on Towi Island, but we didn't give up looking for you. Your brothers distributed fliers and ran advertisements on radio and television stations, hoping someone would recognize you. Your father even offered reward money. We came up empty-handed despite our best efforts. We looked for you for months, but we couldn't find you."

Vanessa sobbed while hugging her mother. She attempted to console her, mumbling that she was safe and back home now, and that they should be thankful they were together again. Martha fixed her gaze on her daughter. Something was different about her, and it was pleasant. She couldn't believe how calm and sweet her daughter was when she spoke to her. When she saw her smile, her heart jumped with joy. If there had been any changes in her daughter's personality, they had been for the better.

What was visible to Vanessa's parents and everyone around her was her attitude: she had changed. Vanessa had grown more relaxed and empathetic toward the sentiments of others. She even helped in the kitchen and made dinner. Vanessa was a big hit with everyone. They enjoyed everything she cooked.

What they didn't realize was that Vanessa was miserable. Everyone seemed preoccupied, and no one noticed her sadness. Everything she did was staged. Vanessa always put on a cheerful smile when she was around them. Her performance fooled everyone who saw nothing amiss. Nobody knew she was heartbroken about the loss of her love. Even after everything he'd done to her, she still loved Michael. When she was alone, she wandered in the garden and sobbed hopelessly for him. She assumed Michael had abandoned her.

He never attempted to contact me. He did not call or come to the hospital to see me. I believe he was merely trying to play me for a fool. He was seeking retaliation for what I had done to him. Oh, yes, I remember him now. He was the server at the club, and I got him fired. He had a valid reason for ridiculing me. I deserved it. I was unkind to him.

Her voice trailed off, but she knew she loved him despite everything.

Where are you, Michael? What are you doing right now? Are you, like me, depressed and lonely? Michael, I'm missing you too. Perhaps you'd completely forgotten about me. Do you know where I am?

· · ✿ · ·

CARMEN, THE GRANDEVILLE'S cook, entered Vanessa's room one morning with a tray of food and placed it on a table next to the bed. She opened the curtains to allow in more light. Vanessa blinked her eyes wide, attempting to block out the sunshine. Carmen shook with fright.

"I-I'm sorry, ma'am. I didn't mean to wake you up. I thought you needed some sunlight in your room."

"Don't worry, Carmen. That was thoughtful of you. Thank you."

Vanessa's comments surprised Carmen. It was the first time she heard her utter "thank you."

"I got you your favorite breakfast. I suspected you were hungry. Is there anything else you want me to get?"

"No, thank you, Carmen. I'm OK."

Vanessa paused for a moment.

"Carmen, I'm sorry I behaved badly before. I'm not sure how you put up with me for so long. I mistreated you, and yet you stayed with me. You didn't leave me."

Carmen let out a chuckle.

"Thank you for your apology, ma'am!"

Vanessa nodded and tried to smile, but missing Michael brought back the sorrow on her sad face.

"Ma'am, if you don't mind my asking, are you okay?"

Vanessa raised her head. She remained silent for a minute, unsure of how to answer. She didn't respond, instead wiping away the trembling tears on her eyelids.

Carmen sensed Vanessa wanted to be alone and left the room, only to come back a few minutes later.

"Your friends are waiting for you downstairs. Should I tell them to come back or let them come up?"

"What do you think?"

"Ma'am? Are you seeking my advice?"

"Yes, Carmen. Do you think it's time for me to go on with my life?"

"Yes, ma'am. It's time to mend your broken heart. You need to be around your friends, those who care about you."

"You are right, Carmen. I've been cooped up in the house for far too long; it's time to get out and have some fun. Yes, please send my friends in. I'm so happy to see them. I'll need to freshen up first, but please send them in."

"Yes, ma'am," Carmen said.

Stephanie, Jennifer, Rachel, Samantha, and Alexandra were overjoyed to see Vanessa. The friends hugged and sobbed. They spoke about things, and it kept Vanessa up to date on some gossip while she was away. It didn't take them long to notice subtle changes in Vanessa's demeanor and viewpoint, just as Carmen and everyone else had. But they knew she had gone through a difficult situation. Time would tell when she would return to her old self again. They had to admit they liked the new Vanessa, especially her cooking skills, which they appreciated very much.

One day, Vanessa joined her mother at a charity event at the children's shelter. She noticed some children playing soccer. Vanessa sat in the bleachers and watched them play. She remembered the kids on Towi Island who had made her happy. It was the first time they made her feel at peace. It was a wonderful feeling, and she would never forget it. Suddenly, she became dizzy and nauseated.

"Miss, are you feeling alright?" a youngster asked.

Vanessa gave him a kind grin. Then she fainted.

. . ⌘ . .

VANESSA BLINKED OPEN her eyes. She scowled as she realized she was back in an unknown environment. She wanted to get up, but her private nurse stopped her.

"Who are you? Where am I?" she inquired.

"You're at Cedarglen Hospital. You passed out early yesterday."

"How long have I been here?"

"You were out of it, ma'am. You've been here for roughly twelve hours."

"Twelve hours? What happened?"

"The doctor should be here any minute. He'll explain everything to you. In the meantime, I'll go get your food. You must be famished."

Vanessa nodded as she watched the nurse go away.

Meanwhile, Martha and Tom were outside her room, speaking with the doctor.

"Vanessa is fine. Her blood pressure is normal. She will be OK, but I am hesitant to discharge her," the doctor added.

"What do you mean?" Tom asked.

"There might be other reasons why she fainted. We took the blood samples, and the results should be available in a day or two."

Tom stroked the back of his neck. "What do you think we should do in the meantime? Our daughter has gone through a lot."

"That's why I'm concerned about releasing her too soon. At least, if she's here, I can assess her condition and provide her with the best viable treatment."

"What exactly are you saying, Dr. Alvarez?" asked Tom, frowning in confusion.

"She may appear in great spirits on the surface, but she is not on the inside. She pretended to be alright, so you wouldn't worry, but she wasn't."

Tom and Martha exchanged a glance. What if the doctor was correct, and Vanessa was merely putting up a brave and happy face for them, but when she was alone, she was miserable?

"I am not an expert in this kind of situation, and I make no claim to be one, but your daughter is not in a healthy mental state. I'm concerned about her stress level. Something is troubling her. She needs to be in a place where she can rest," the doctor said.

"Perhaps it's time for us to take a vacation. I'm thinking about Italy—Vanessa's favorite spot. We haven't been there in a long time. We have a vineyard there, and it's the perfect place for her to unwind," Tom explained. "Dr. Alvarez, if you give her permission to travel, we will depart as quickly as possible."

The doctor was quiet, as though pondering Tom's comments. "Hmm, maybe that's a good idea. A relaxing vacation in Italy would brighten her spirits."

"OK, doctor. We'll depart tonight. We want our daughter to recover, and we will go to whatever lengths to make it happen. If you need us, just call us in Italy. Here's my business card."

Dr. Alvarez released Vanessa, and when they arrived home, Tom phoned his secretary to make their vacation plans. He canceled all his meetings until they returned.

.. ⚜ ..

VANESSA SAT NEAR THE window, gazing out as the rain fell. She adored their villa's breathtaking view of the vineyards.

Italy is the ideal honeymoon destination for Michael and me. I should bring him here one of these days.

"Do you need anything, sweetheart?" Martha spoke in hushed tones.

Vanessa faced her mother and murmured quietly, "I'm sorry, Mom. I didn't hear you come in."

Martha sat on the windowsill next to Vanessa.

"Are you sure you're all right, baby? You know, you can tell me what's bothering you."

"Yes, mother, I know. I'm just tired. I need some rest."

"I'll be downstairs if you need anything."

Vanessa nodded as her mother stepped out the door, closing it behind her.

The phone rang at 10:17 p.m. Except for Tom, who was reading a book in the library, everyone was asleep. He scowled and checked his watch.

Who would call so late?

The phone rang again for a few seconds, before ceasing to ring. When the phone rang again, Tom let out an irritated groan. He got up from his chair and picked up the phone.

"Hello? Who is this?" he enragedly inquired.

"This is Dr. Alvarez, Mr. Grandeville."

"Oh yes, doctor, what can I do for you?"

"I apologize, Mr. Grandeville. Did I wake you?"

"Oh, no, not at all. I was reading a book."

"I couldn't wait to break the news to Vanessa. May I speak to her?"

Tom said, "She's already in bed. What is this all about?"

"According to Vanessa's file, she signed the proper consent form to release her medical information to you. Therefore, it's okay for me to tell you, Mr. Grandeville."

"Tell me what?"

"We received Vanessa's blood test results. Everything is normal, except your daughter is four months pregnant."

There was silence on the other end of the telephone. It took Tom by surprise and left him speechless.

"Are you still there, Mr. Grandeville? Hello?"

"Yes, I'm still here," he said, nearly in hushed tones.

"I understand this is shocking news, Mr. Grandeville."

"Yes, it is. I still can't believe it. My daughter is expecting a child."

"In her condition, it's critical that she rest, eat nutritious foods, and avoid situations that may cause her unnecessary stress," Dr. Alvarez said. "How long will you be in Italy?"

"We were planning on staying indefinitely, but now I think our plan has changed. Thank you, Dr. Alvarez," Tom remarked. "I appreciate your concern for my daughter's health."

"Just take good care of her. I'll see you all when you return to Los Angeles."

"Yes, Dr. Alvarez. We'll see you then," he murmured before hanging up.

Tom put down the phone and buried his face in his hands. It was too difficult to take it all in at once. He had a stunned expression on his face. He couldn't believe it. There weren't enough words to explain how much he feared telling Martha and Vanessa the truth. He was shocked to see Martha standing behind him.

"Tom, who was on the phone?"

Tom exhaled a big, shaky breath and sighed.

"It was Dr. Alvarez."

"Calling at this hour? What did he want?"

"Well, um... "

"Tom?" Martha asked, her gaze fixed on him.

Tom paused for a time, unsure of how to respond to her. "Martha, I don't know how to say this."

Martha waited for Tom to say something, but when he didn't, she spoke up.

"For God's sake, Tom, say it already!"

"Dr. Alvarez called to let me know they received the blood test results. Her pregnancy caused Vanessa's sickness," Tom remarked.

"Vanessa is pregnant?" Martha asked, surprised.

"I'm afraid so. Four months to be exact."

There was an unpleasant silence between them. Martha looked at Tom as if she asked him what they should do. Vanessa's voice from behind them startled them.

"I'm pregnant?" Vanessa murmured as she caressed her stomach. "I'm going to be a mother?"

Tom and Martha remained deafeningly silent, unable to fathom what had occurred. For the first time, they watched their daughter genuinely smile, her eyes welling up with tears of joy. Vanessa was giddy with delight.

"I know you think I ruined my life, but you are mistaken. I was pretty messed up before I had the amnesia. I was disrespectful to others and didn't care what they thought of me. I didn't care if I stepped on anyone's toes, since all I cared about was getting what I wanted. I'm going to have a baby with the man I love. I wish you could believe that I have never been happier than I am right now. Michael is only a fisherman, and I know you won't like him, but I love him. He taught me to love, be sensitive, and be a better person. To tell you the truth, I miss him terribly. The Michael I know wouldn't let anything awful happen to me. He would never forsake me. I'm sure he has a good reason why he never tried to see me at the hospital."

Tom could tell where this was going. With each exhalation, he became more enraged. He couldn't bear the notion of Vanessa's reputation being tarnished. Tom hid his face in his hands. It was too much for him to take in all at once, but eventually calmed down. For a while, they were deafeningly silent.

"I'm sorry, Mom and Dad. But I'm heading back to Towi Island. Michael and I are about to have a baby, and I wish you could see how content I am with my life. I'm hoping you'll be happy for me."

"All right," Tom finally responded. "You are right, Vanessa. You've changed. You are now a better person than you were previously. We are proud of you for maturing into a responsible adult. For a long time, we hated ourselves for allowing you to get away with so much. We believed we had raised a tyrant. Your mom and I thought we were irresponsible parents, because we let you walk all over us and spoil you."

"Dad—"

"No, let me finish, please," Tom said. "We're not getting any younger. Your mother and I were discussing the other night if we'd live long enough to see our grandchildren before the Almighty God took us. And now we know we'll be around to witness the birth of our first grandchild."

Vanessa looked up, taken by surprise.

"Do you mean that, Dad? Are you okay with having a fisherman as a son-in-law?"

"Vanessa, I, too, was once a small-town kid. Your grandparents farmed. We didn't start off rich. We were destitute before we were wealthy. I have nothing against fishermen, salespeople, or busboys. They're all good jobs, and as long as this Michael person makes you happy, then we're okay with it."

"Oh, thank you so much, Dad. Right now, you're brightening my day. If you don't mind, I'd like to return to Towi Island where I belong. I want to go home and be with my husband. Please trust me when I say I have never been happier or more content in my life. Michael completes me."

Tom took a deep breath before speaking.

"Vanessa, there is something you should know. I hired a private investigator and a couple of bodyguards to keep an eye on Michael and report back to me. He tried to see you at the hospital on Towi Island, and we fooled him into thinking you were still there. All the while, we were in Honolulu. When he found out we'd already left the island, it was too late, but he saw you board our private plane bound for Los Angeles. He lingered outside the gate until after we had departed. Vanessa, please accept my apologies for not telling you the truth. We thought what we were doing was for your own good. We won't object if you go back to Michael if he makes you happy."

"I knew it. I had a feeling Michael would never desert me. Thank you so much, Dad and Mom, for telling me the truth. Now, if you excuse me, I have some packing to do. It's time for me to go home."

"I can't believe we will be grandparents," said Tom as he hugged his wife.

Vanessa joined them, tears flowing down their cheeks.

"I'll notify our pilot to get ready." Tom said.

"Would you like to come with me, Mom and Dad? I want you to meet Michael. I want you to get to know the man that captured my heart."

Tom and Martha exchanged grins.

"Even if you didn't invite us to accompany you, we were planning to go. We need to be there to apologize to Michael and welcome him into our family, if that's what you desire."

Vanessa grinned.

"That's exactly what I want, Mom."

"Well, let's get moving then, shall we?"

Vanessa couldn't wait to return to Towi Island. She couldn't wait to see Michael's handsome face. She was nervous about telling him they were going to have a baby. How would he respond to the news? Would he still love her?

They quickly boarded their own jet. Before takeoff, Tom's secretary called to say there was an emergency board meeting in Los Angeles and that they needed to adjust their travel itinerary. Tom informed Vanessa that she would have to wait a little longer until the meeting was over, but Vanessa couldn't wait to see Michael. She told her parents that she would take a commercial airline to Honolulu. Tom nodded, saying they'd meet her there as soon as possible.

They landed at a private airport fourteen and a half hours later. Tom's secretary was there to greet them. She handed Vanessa her boarding pass. She secured the last business-class ticket to Honolulu. Vanessa kissed her parents goodbye and stepped into a limousine ready to take her to Los Angeles International Airport.

CHAPTER EIGHTEEN

Michael woke up early, feeling excited. He showered and dressed. He entered the lobby and headed to the coffee shop for breakfast. Michael saw Mario stroll in a moment later. He grimaced and checked his watch—it was 7:00 a.m.

"Hey Mario, are you just getting in?" he said as he paid for his breakfast. "I thought we were going to see celebrity houses today."

"Alberto doesn't arrive until 10 a.m. I have two more hours to work until I clock out," Mario replied, smiling, then frowning when he glanced at Michael from head to toe.

"Wait a second. Are you wearing a shirt, shorts, and slippers?"

"Well, yes. What's wrong with the way I'm dressed?"

"It's OK if you're in Hawaii, but you're in Los Angeles. We need to blend in with the crowd as if we were locals. You know what I mean? You don't want to appear a tourist."

"But I am a tourist."

"Yeah, I know, but..."

"But what? What do you suggest?"

"Let me call my other cousin, Jose. He owns a men's clothing store a few blocks from here. Leave everything to me, OK?"

"I guess."

"Don't guess. I'll take care of you, my brother. Trust me," said Mario, chuckling. "Go back to your room, and I'll meet you later."

Michael nodded and mounted the stairs to go to his room. He fell asleep until there was a knock at the door. He looked at the clock on the nightstand. It was 9:15 a.m. He opened the door, and Mario walked in wearing a nice polo shirt and slacks.

"Here you go, my friend. Go change," said Mario, as he handed him two bags. "My cousin, Jose, dropped it off here. I am sure they'll fit you."

Michael took the bags with apprehension, before stepping into the bathroom. He emerged a few minutes later, wearing Levi jeans, a white t-shirt, and Van sneakers.

"Wow, man! You look like a movie star. I never imagined a gorgeous man lurking under that tanned face and bleached hair."

"Shut up, Mario. That is not funny. I wear these kinds of clothes in Hawaii, too, you know? I was in a hurry to get here and packed everything without thinking."

"OK, but I'm telling you the truth, dude! You look awesome. If I wasn't a guy, I'd fall in love with you," Mario joked.

Michael picked up a bed pillow and flung it towards Mario, who laughed as he dodged it.

· · ⌘ · ·

IT'S 10 A.M. THE JUST Trippin' Tour Bus pulled up in front of the Beverly Hills Mega Resort. The bus was packed. As soon as he got on the bus, Mario hugged his cousin Alberto. He introduced Michael, who shook Alberto's hand. As they were departing, Alberto told them to take their seats. He pointed to a reserved seat behind him.

"How many cousins do you have, Mario?" asked Michael, chuckling.

"Don't ask," Mario replied with a laugh. "Hey Alberto, do you ever stop by the Grandeville residence?"

"Grandeville? Oh, yeah. It's in Beverly Hills. Yes, that's where we're going. It's our last stop before heading back."

Michael was pleased to learn Alberto knew where the Grandeville's lived, but it disappointed him that it was the last stop. It meant he'd have to wait two hours longer to see Vanessa.

The journey began in the heart of Hollywood. Alberto provided comments as they traveled around the city. Michael remained seated, and all he cared about was getting to the last stop. His thoughts were fixed on one person and one person only—Vanessa.

The tour bus finally arrived in Beverly Hills after what seemed like a lifetime. The houses they passed were massive and gorgeous, with planted gardens that seemed to compete. Everyone on the tour bus took pictures with their cameras. They were hoping to get a peek at a star.

"The prominent Grandeville family lives within the gated neighborhood." Alberto announced the PA system of the bus.

Michael's eyes widened with excitement. He craned his neck, hoping to get a glimpse inside the fence.

At long last, I'm here! Michael wanted to scream. *I'm here, sweetie!*

The tour bus proceeded down the next block. Michael said to Mario, "I'll get off the bus and jump the fence to get to Vanessa's house."

"That's suicide, man! That place is a fortress."

"I'd want to see Vanessa. I can't give up now."

"I know, but you have to have a plan. You can't just walk in. You'll wind up in prison. Besides, we don't even know their specific address, and if you missed it, there's a security officer at the gate."

"We spent two hours on the bus, Mario, and you want us to turn around and go home? We are so close."

"At the very least, we now know where they live. You must devise a brilliant plan to gain entry without raising suspicion."

"What do you recommend I do?"

"Take me out for a drink, and I'm sure I'll come up with something."

• • ❧ • •

THE POOL SERVICE TRUCK arrived at the luxury guarded estate early in the morning, driven by yet another of Mario's cousins, Hector. He was working on the house next to the Grandeville mansion. Hector proceeded inside the home to a covered terrace that led to a kidney-shaped pool in the backyard. Meanwhile, Michael scouted the area, easily getting over the high walls and trees and inside the Grandeville property. He had a lot of experience climbing trees in Towi. Scaling barriers was a piece of cake.

The Grandevilles' home had the most magnificent garden, full of flowers and large trees. Their mansion was enormous—twenty times bigger than Towi's only hotel. Michael hid in the shrubs' shadows. He dashed through the open garage, hiding behind the five expensive automobiles. Michael listened for any sounds, but heard none. He sneaked up to the garage entrance door and was ready to open it when he heard a dog bark from within, and it sounded agitated. Michael trembled as he climbed back over the wall.

He was panting when he saw Hector by the pool next door. Michael assisted him with his work, hoping to get a glimpse of Vanessa in the backyard. He surveyed the Grandeville's vast garden from the top of the diving board, but all he saw were tall trees and a well-kept lawn. Vanessa was nowhere to be seen.

"I understand what you're going through, but you need to get a grip." Hector tried to comfort him, but his words seemed more like a mockery, saying, "You look like a lost dog! Get your act together!"

Michael gave a heavy sigh.

The maid then brought out a pitcher of lemonade.

"I thought you and your friend may be thirsty," she remarked, giving Hector goo-goo looks. Hector noticed it right away.

"You have such gorgeous eyes, Rosie," he said.

The maid flushed.

"How long have you been working with the Williams family?" Hector inquired; his voice amused.

"It'll be my sixth year here on Monday. Why do you ask?"

"Then I'm sure you know the ones who live next door."

"Which house? The Grandeville or the Hudson?"

"Grandeville!" Michael exclaimed, his eyes gleaming with hope and excitement.

"What about them?"

"Nothing. We're just curious, that's all," Hector said as he took her hand in his.

Rosie drew her hand back, a smile on her face. She then returned his gaze. She watched as Hector leaned against the wall, one hand in his pocket and the other holding his jacket over his shoulder, posing like James Dean. His carefree demeanor drew Rosie in. Hector knew how to play and what he was doing.

Rosie responded with a flirty smile.

"Well, I will not gossip, but Carmen, their chef, informed me that her boss departed a few days ago with their daughter for Italy. Only the two sons are home."

"Italy?" Michael screamed in fear.

"Yes, Italy. They'll be there indefinitely," Rosie said.

Michael was heartbroken to get the news.

"It's not supposed to be like this. We are soul mates. Two hearts intended to be together! Italy is far away and vast. I'm not sure where to look for you there, Vanessa!" he screamed, squeezing his hand to his chest.

"What's wrong with your friend?" Rosie asked, her brows furrowed.

Hector shook his head. "I don't know," he answered.

Michael stepped out of the gated neighborhood, his hands in his pockets and his head down, staring at the ground. His mind was racing.

"Michael!" Hector yelled out to him while driving his vehicle beside him, but Michael continued to walk without looking at him.

"C'mon, dude. Let me take you back to your hotel. It's time to go home."

Michael murmured, "Home."

He decided it was best if he returned home to Towi Island, where he belonged. Michael accepted defeat. Vanessa hailed from a wealthy family, and even if he found her, her parents would do everything they could to keep her away from him.

Michael stood in front of the iron gates and yelled, "This is the hardest thing I've ever done, but it's time to set you free, Vanessa! I will treasure the memories we shared. Vanessa Florence Grandeville, thank you for everything. I will love you forever!"

The guards glanced at him, clicked their tongues, and exclaimed, "Weirdo!" before asking him to move away from the gate.

Hector drove Michael back to his hotel and waved farewell before departing. Michael took the elevator to the second floor and went inside his room, locking the door behind him. He gathered his belongings and placed them in his travel bag. Michael took another look around the room to ensure he had forgotten nothing. He sat on the bed, pondering his next move. His decision to leave was the best choice, because there was nothing else for him to do there.

Michael checked out of his hotel room and hailed a cab to the airport. When he arrived, he checked in at the airline desk for the first available flight back to Honolulu. The ticketing agent checked her computer and informed Michael that the last flight to Honolulu for the day was leaving in an hour. They're going to board soon. Business-class tickets were already sold out, and they booked all economy seats except for one at the tail of the plane, near lavatories or a galley. Michael didn't care where he sat, so he took it. All he wanted was to curl up in a cave and vanish. The rear of the plane was perfect for him, since he wanted to hide from the rest of the world.

.. ❧ ..

VANESSA MADE HER WAY to the business-class lounge, but she couldn't stop thinking about Michael. What she needed was to keep her mind occupied, or she would go insane thinking about and missing him.

A few more hours till I see you, my love, she moaned.

Vanessa looked around and noticed a gift shop nearby. She walked in through the rotating door, while Michael walked out through the double doors, escorting a thin, graying, frail-looking old woman clutching his arm. He was assisting her in carrying her bags. She almost passed out at the gift shop because she forgot to take her medication. Michael was behind her in line when he noticed she was going to fall. He'd caught her before she fell to the ground.

"Son," the old woman said, her voice fainting. "Did anybody ever tell you how lucky your parents are to have raised such a wonderful young man?"

Michael broke out in a wide grin.

"No, ma'am. You're the first one," he stated as he handed her bags back to her when they arrived at the gate's waiting area. Her husband came to greet them. Michael wrapped his arms around the elderly woman, before kissing her wrinkled cheek. The old woman reached into her purse and tried to give Michael a few dollars.

"Oh no, ma'am. I was happy to assist you. There's no need to reward me."

"Young man, if I were unmarried and younger, I would marry you right here," the elderly lady said while her husband chuckled.

"And if you were single, I would marry you right here, right now," Michael teased. The elderly woman held his face in her hands before hugging Michael.

Meanwhile, Vanessa mostly flipped through the pages of a magazine, oblivious to its contents. When the gate agent announced it was time to board the plane moments later, calling the business-class passengers first, Vanessa dashed out of the store.

Before calling the people in economy class, Michael hurried to the restroom. Vanessa and the others had already boarded the plane when he returned to the gate, missing each other again.

A flight attendant escorted Vanessa to her seat. They placed her belongings in the overhead bin. Vanessa freshened up and walked inside the business-class lavatory, while everyone else was busy putting their things away. Michael eventually boarded the plane, headed for the economy section, and walked right by everyone in the business class section with his head down and without looking. If he had, he would have seen Vanessa exit the lavatory and return to her seat. They missed each other by a second, yet again. The plane took off without either of them realizing they were on the same plane.

• • ❧ • •

THE FLIGHT WAS FIVE hours long. Vanessa was restless, while the other business-class passengers were comfortable and well rested because of the luxuries and outstanding service they received. Vanessa stayed seated as her fellow passengers social-ized in the on-board lounge, and she would only get up if she needed to use the restroom.

Michael, who was sitting in economy class at the back of the plane, couldn't control his emotions and had tears in his eyes. He tried to be strong, but he couldn't ignore the fact that he knew he'd never see Vanessa again.

"Excuse me, sir. We'll be arriving shortly. Please fasten your seatbelt."

The pleasant voice of the flight attendant interrupted Michael's thoughts and brought him back to reality. He looked around, disoriented.

The plane landed safely. Business class passengers were the first to disembark without coming into contact with any of the passengers in the other sections. By the time Michael arrived at the baggage claim to get his luggage, Vanessa had already been picked up by the limousine driver to take her to the Paradise Tower in Waikiki, where she had intended to stay overnight—the hotel where her lovely story with Michael had begun.

Michael flagged down a taxi to take him to Ernesto's to thank him and say his goodbyes. He entered through Paradise Tower's rotating door, while Vanessa had exited the same door, looking down, fumbling through her handbag, searching for her cell phone. Thus, missing each other again.

Vanessa met with the contractor she hired to build a nurs-ery room for their expectant child. She wanted it to be a sur-prise for Michael. She wanted everything to be perfect, and it took her many hours to finish the plan, but she was happy with the changes she made.

CHAPTER NINETEEN

Vanessa arrived on Towi Island early the next morning. She returned to the house she had shared with Michael, but it appeared desolate, as if no one had lived there for a long time. Vanessa peered through the window, but saw no one inside. She couldn't enter since she didn't have a key. Vanessa walked to her restaurant, which had a heavy coating of dust covering the doors and windows. There were even newspapers piled up at the front door. Michael had lost his desire to live.

Where could he possibly be?

Vanessa expected Michael to return home at some point. She walked back to the house and waited for him. Vanessa kept herself busy by pulling stubborn weeds in her garden and picking up dead leaves. An hour had passed, and there was no sign of Michael. She felt agitated and decided to visit Sophia. Vanessa was on her way to see her when she remembered a special place Michael often went to relax. As she reflected on this, she grew enthralled and took off running as fast as she could.

Michael was crying as he sat on the trunk of his beloved coconut tree, drinking away his sorrows. He couldn't forgive himself for letting Vanessa leave. In despair, he was weeping and sobbing aloud.

"Michael!"

Michael thought he was daydreaming. He kept hearing Vanessa's voice. He didn't know how he got through the days without her.

"Oh, Vanessa, I miss you so much."

"Michael!"

Michael heard his name called again and again, and each time the voice got clearer. It was not his imagination. He was certain it was Vanessa's voice. When he turned around, he saw Vanessa running towards him. His eyes widened. He raced over to her, wrapped his arms around her, and held her, swinging her around and around. They both couldn't stop laughing. He kissed her, sending her body on fire with his touch.

"Vanessa, you've returned!" He kissed her again, with the longing and love he felt.

Vanessa gave Michael a sidelong glance. He'd gone through a dramatic shift in appearance and demeanor. He neglected himself, allowing his beard to grow out. She noticed new wrinkles on his forehead and frown lines around his eyes. He looked tired, as if he hadn't slept in a long time.

"Oh, Michael, what have I done? I'm sorry I left you. Will you forgive me? I promise I will never leave you again."

"My darling, Vanessa. Do you know how many times I felt I was going insane from wanting to see you these past few months?" He muttered, his lips brushing across her face. He took a step closer to her, his pulse hammering as he kissed her on the cheek, then across her face and to her lips. Vanessa couldn't believe she was in his arms again. She stood on her toes and leaned forward, her entire body shaking; a bolt of lightning was rushing through her as his touch made her feel like every part of her was alive. Her veins were tingling with excitement. Her stomach tightened.

"Vanessa, please don't do it again. When you left, it seemed like someone had reached into my chest and pulled my heart out. Never ever leave me again!" Michael pleaded.

"I promise," she said as she caressed her stomach.

"Michael, I have something to tell you."

"What is it?" Michael responded, but continued to hold her.

"Sweetheart, we're going to have a baby!"

"A baby? Are you sure?"

"Yes, we're going to be parents in five months."

"Do you mean you were expecting when you left Towi Island?"

"I suppose so," Vanessa chuckled.

"Yahoo!" Michael said as he hugged and kissed her.

Vanessa fell silent and caught Michael's stare. She grabbed his hand in hers, elevating it and laying it on her chest.

"I'd like to marry you for real, Michael. That is why I came all the way here to tell you." Her voice was full of emotion. "I came back to tell you how much I love you, and to inform you that we will have a baby."

Michael wrapped her in his arms and embraced her closely, as if he didn't want to let her go.

"Yes, we will marry as soon as possible."

He paused for a moment to reflect.

"I must be dreaming," he remarked, feeling like the happiest guy on the earth. He then sat Vanessa down, cupped her face in his hands, and, to her amazement, knelt on his knees.

"We have to do this right. I'd been holding this ring for a long time, waiting for the perfect moment to propose to you, but as you know, life happens. Now, my lady, I kneel before you as a humble fisherman in love with you. Will you, Vanessa Florence Grandeville, grant me the honor of being my wife for real? To love me and make me the happiest man alive for as long as we both shall live. "

Vanessa couldn't stop the tears falling down her cheeks. She wiped her eyes and kissed Michael, before saying, "Yes, yes, yes! I will marry you!"

Vanessa cried as Michael placed the ring on her finger. She had long yearned for this moment. The ring belonged to Michael's mother. His father gave it to him years ago, and he made him promise to give it to the one who would make him happy for the rest of his life. The ring was simple, yet stunning, with tiny sapphires around a large, square diamond in the center. Vanessa thought it was the most beautiful ring she'd ever seen.

Michael leaned forward and kissed her on the lips. As if that wasn't enough, he kissed her cheek again, filled with excitement. Then Michael snatched Vanessa up in his arms and twirled her around again, laughing at the happiness that had grown inside him. Then he grabbed her hand and drove like the wind back to their house. When they arrived, Michael seized Vanessa's arms and kissed her. He then picked her up, never taking his lips away from hers, as he opened the bedroom door, then kicked it shut behind him as they made up for lost time.

A few days later, Vanessa received a call from her mother. They had just landed in Honolulu with her brothers, and were due to arrive on Towi Island in the afternoon. Martha intended to meet them for supper at the hotel where they were staying. Michael grew concerned when Vanessa mentioned meeting her family. He knew he'd have to meet them at some point, but he wasn't prepared, and that made him nervous. He didn't make a favorable impression on Vanessa's family the last time he saw them.

"Don't worry, sweetheart; they'll love you," Vanessa repeatedly reassured him, but Michael felt sick.

Vanessa tried everything she could to comfort Michael, but he was still unconvinced. He had a hunch it was going to be a disaster.

• • ✿ • •

THE DAY SEEMED TO GO on forever. Michael sighed heavily and swallowed hard as he knocked on the front door. He sweated bullets from nervousness. The anxiety was rising by the minute. When Michael tightened his grip on Vanessa's hand, a huge grin appeared on her face.

"Relax, honey. They will not bite you. And why did you have to wear a tie? I've never seen you wear one before. You look as if you are going to a funeral. These are my parents. You don't have to impress them."

Michael whispered to himself as he fixed his tie. *More like an execution, you mean.*

"Did you say something, dear?" Vanessa asked.

"Never mind that. Could we go home and come back another day?"

Vanessa laughed. "Oh, honey, take a deep breath. If you don't relax, you will hyperventilate and pass out."

The maid opened the door. When Michael noticed Jason's doubtful expression as he rose from his chair to extend his hand to him, Michael swallowed hard.

"It's great to finally meet you. Come in," Jason murmured, a strained smile on his face.

He and his twin, TJ, didn't appear to be rolling out the welcome mat. Michael glanced at Jason now, leaning with his arms crossed and watching him in silence.

"How are you, Michael?" TJ asked.

Michael gave him a little grin as he looked up. "I'm OK," he said.

Then he saw Tom and Martha enter the room. Panic erupted inside him, nearly too much to take. Michael became even more concerned when he observed they were wearing solemn looks. He swallowed forcefully once more.

Vanessa kissed her parents and then introduced Michael to the family. With his heart thumping, Michael extended his hand, but he trembled. His knees got weak, and everything went wrong. Michael shook Tom's and Martha's hands, but his palms were sweaty. He pulled his hand away and wiped it on his jeans. Michael felt agitated. He was twitchy and panting. He was a nervous wreck.

"Humph... are you intoxicated, young man?" Tom grunted.

"N-no, sir," he mumbled as he wiped the perspiration from his forehead.

Michael noticed Tom shaking his head as he sighed. Michael loosened his tie and undid two buttons on his shirt, but he still couldn't catch his breath. Vanessa was correct in her assessment. He should not have worn a tie. He nearly collapsed from nervousness, but he took several deep breaths and returned to normal. Michael knew it would be a long night.

Vanessa spoke with her family as Michael sat next to her. He felt out of place, since no one tried to include him in the conversation. Michael was counting the minutes until he could leave. The night wasn't going well for him. The next few minutes were awkward, and he had the impression everyone despised him.

Vanessa excused herself to visit the restroom. The room fell quiet as soon as she left. Vanessa's parents and brothers sat across from Michael, each looking at him with a strange expression. Michael felt a tremble in his insides. He thought he had prepared himself for this moment, but he was mistaken. He was a mess.

"Is there something you wish to tell us, Michael?" Tom said, breaking the stillness.

"Sir, I asked Vanessa to marry me, and she accepted, but I'd want your blessing as well."

"And they claimed I don't have any manners," Tom replied, a small smirk on his face.

"Sir?"

"I thought it was common courtesy to first ask my wife and me, before asking for my daughter's hand in marriage."

Michael thought Tom had a point. He was protective of Vanessa, as any parent would be.

"Um, yes, sir. I realize it's quick, but I was just thinking about the baby and Vanessa. I want to marry your daughter before we have our child."

Michael waited for Tom to speak, but he didn't. He stayed silent for an extended period, which made him anxious again.

Michael sensed they didn't approve of him for Vanessa, and he didn't know what to do or say, since he was too nervous. What could he say to make them like him?

Michael had been trying to read everyone's faces from across the table during supper, but was unsuccessful. The dinner was delicious: steak and a giant lobster, but he couldn't taste it since he was so uncomfortable. He gave up, trying to push himself to eat.

"You didn't enjoy the food?" Tom asked.

"The food is fantastic, sir," Michael responded. He took another mouthful, but Michael was so nervous that he didn't fully chew it and choked. He tried to wash it down with wine, but it didn't work. He was afraid to say anything, but after a few seconds of not breathing, his face grew crimson. Michael broke out in a cold sweat. His head was pounding. He couldn't take it any longer and pointed his finger towards his throat. Vanessa noticed him, and she freaked out.

"Michael, my God, what's the matter?"

Michael continued, pointing his finger towards his throat. He was choking on something.

Jason jumped up and gave Michael the Heimlich technique. The steak flew across the table after a few thrusts against Michael's stomach, striking Tom in the face. Michael threw up on the floor. Everyone had a horrified expression on their faces as he came around. Michael felt it was the most dreadful night of his life.

He went to the restroom to clean up, somewhat reluctantly. No one said anything to him as he returned to the dining room and sat down, as if nothing had occurred. He could feel everyone staring at him, trying to find even the slightest fault.

Michael forced a grin as he pulled his chair back and rose to excuse himself. He walked away from the table and into the washroom again, without looking back. Michael paced. Should he go back? Should he leave? He felt as if it were his last supper before being executed.

When he returned to the dinner table for the second time, he noticed how quiet it was. He scowled. He peered through the door, and it surprised him to find that everyone had left, except for the maid that the Grandeville had hired while they were vacationing on Towi Island. She was clearing the table.

"Did you see which way they went?" he inquired of the maid.

"No, sir. I'm sorry."

Michael panicked.

Where did they go? Where is my wife? I hope they don't take Vanessa from me again.

He dashed outside, hoping Vanessa had returned to their home, but what if she hadn't? What if her family said they didn't like him? Michael became terrified by the prospect. The thought of losing Vanessa again sent shivers down his spine. He leaned back on the wooden railing in despair, but he lost his balance. Michael flung his arms forward and tossed his head back. He landed mostly on soft ground. Michael stood up. He looked around and exhaled with relief when he realized no one had seen him fall. He was on his way to his pickup when he heard someone call his name.

"Michael!"

He glanced in the voice's direction and saw Vanessa, her parents, and brothers, sitting on a swing, laughing. They witnessed everything.

"Are you all right? Do you think you need to go to the hospital?" Tom asked, concerned.

"No need, sir. It's just a scratch," Michael responded, his cheeks flushed with embarrassment.

"We're sorry for what happened back there, Michael. We were just having fun with you. That's how we'd want to welcome you to our family. I hope we didn't scare you!" Jason stated.

"Yeah, we're sorry, dude! We were trying to figure out how to welcome you into the family and decided to put on an act to see what would happen. When Vanessa understood it was a prank, she played along with us," TJ explained.

"I'm sorry, honey. I couldn't help myself from seeing you in action, but you scared us to death when you were choking. Dad was on the phone dialing 9-1-1 when a chunk of steak smacked him in the face," Vanessa laughed.

"I apologize for the steak, sir. I think I didn't chew it thoroughly. And, Jason, you did not frighten me. I knew you were playing me the whole time," Michael said, wiping perspiration from his forehead.

"I could tell, honey. As cool as a cucumber," Vanessa remarked, and everyone laughed.

"We would love to have you as a member of our family, Michael. We don't have much choice," Tom said.

"Dad!" Vanessa said, trying to quiet her father. "Don't listen to him, Michael; they love you."

"All right, Michael, we love you. Welcome to the family," Tom exclaimed, as everyone embraced Michael.

"Tell us the truth, Michael. Did we frighten you?" Martha inquired.

"The truth, ma'am? I was so terrified I almost peed my pants," Michael remarked, stifling a giggle.

Everyone burst out laughing.

"Welcome to the family, son. Let's go to the bar and have a drink," Tom said, and everyone agreed.

It was a night Michael would never forget. Vanessa's family accepted him and even agreed to their marriage. As they walked into their house, Michael cupped Vanessa's face in his hands.

"I love you, my spoiled princess, with all my heart. I've loved you from the first time I saw you," Michael said as he wrapped his arm around her, drew her closer, and kissed her on the lips. "I promise to..."

Vanessa hushed him with her own kiss.

"And I love you with all my heart and soul."

CHAPTER TWENTY

Vanessa and Michael were in Honolulu looking for a ready-to-wear wedding gown. There was no time to have a custom-made gown by a well-known designer, since Michael pressed on getting married over the same weekend. He was excited about starting their new life together as a married couple.

Vanessa checked the bridal stores in Honolulu while Michael waited outside. She had no luck finding the perfect dress for herself. She assumed shopping for a ready-made wedding gown would be simple, but it was tiring. Vanessa tried on dress after dress, but none of them looked or felt right. She was becoming agitated. Vanessa wasn't sure what she was searching for, but as she passed a modest wedding boutique around the corner, she knew she had to try on the white lace dress on the window display. She asked Michael to buy her a cheeseburger and fries from a nearby hamburger stand while she checked out the dress.

Vanessa stood there for a long time, gazing at the bridal gown. She hoped it was her size. The salesperson removed the garment from the mannequin and pointed Vanessa toward the fitting room.

Vanessa buttoned up her dress and headed outside to check herself in a large mirror. She spun around, admiring the silky-smooth cloth that stroked across her skin. It highlighted every curve of her body, as if it were tailor-made for her. She simply needed a few minor changes to make it great.

"You look wonderful," said the saleslady.

"Thank you. This is the outfit I've been looking for. I can't believe I discovered that in your store."

"I'm glad you like it. It was a unique design, a one-of-a-kind gown. My mother had made it before becoming ill. She intended to create it in five sizes, but she had to go on bed rest before she could."

"Oh, I'm sorry to hear that."

"The doctor instructed her to take a relaxing vacation, but we couldn't afford it with medical bills and a slowing economy. She's home resting."

Vanessa felt pity for the girl and her mother. Vanessa wrote a ten-thousand-dollar check for the dress, as the clerk was busy placing her bridal gown in a white box. When she handed the check to the clerk, it shocked her. She was speechless when she saw the amount written on it. After her initial shock faded to bemusement, she took a deep breath, and the clerk finally found her voice.

"Ma'am, this is too much," the saleslady said. "This check is worth more than the value of our inventory. I cannot accept this. The gown was only $500."

"Believe me, this is a steal. As you stated, this is a one-of-a-kind gown. And with that money, I'm sure you'll afford your mother the therapy she requires, while still having extra cash to help you with your business."

Vanessa had a brilliant idea.

"Better yet, I'd like to make you and your mother a business offer. Your mom is a fantastic seamstress and designer. Maybe we can talk about a business collaboration when she gets better? Here's my business card. Just call me later, okay?"

When the saleslady saw the name on the card, she sobbed.

"Grandeville? Oh, my goodness! I don't know what to say. You are an angel."

"I'm not sure about that, but you gave me the best wedding present ever. This dress is beautiful and perfect for a pregnant bride. Please thank your mother for me and tell her to get well. I look forward to hearing from her soon."

The clerk was overwhelmed with appreciation. She thanked Vanessa for her generosity and the business opportunity. She said her mother would finally get the medical treatment she needed. The clerk gave Vanessa a gentle hug of appreciation, and Vanessa waved to her as she left.

Michael was sitting on a bench holding a food bag containing two cheeseburgers and French fries for Vanessa when he saw her walking towards him carrying a large white box. He smiled at her and asked if everything was all right.

"Everything is perfect, sweetheart; just perfect!" Vanessa said with a wide-open smile. "Guess what? I finally found my wedding dress!"

"Thank goodness," Michael sighed with relief.

After walking a short distance, Michael and Vanessa entered a Japanese restaurant. They met Vanessa's parents and brothers for dinner. They were also in Honolulu, shopping for their clothes for the wedding. Vanessa told Michael to get a quiet table by the fountain while she headed to the ladies' room to powder her nose.

"What should I do with these cheeseburgers?" he asked as he lifted the food bag higher.

"Don't worry, sweetheart. I'll eat mine with my sushi."

Michael was shocked. Vanessa's pregnancy gave her such an incredible appetite. He scratched his head as he watched his wife walk away.

"Good evening, Michael," greeted the manager.

"Hello, Akio. I didn't know you worked here."

Akio worked at Ernesto's.

"My father-in-law bought this place, and I manage it now. By the way, I will be a father soon."

"No kidding! My wife is pregnant too. That reminds me. I need a quiet table over by the fountain for six. We are meeting my in-laws here."

"Excellent, sir. This way, please."

When Michael followed Akio to the table, he heard a familiar voice calling him.

"Michael, hey, Michael. Over here!" Sharon screamed.

Michael turned around, surprised to see Sharon and her sisters sitting at the next table with a male friend.

Vanessa came out of the ladies' room and broke into a broad smile when she saw Sharon dining with her sisters, Sherice and Sheryl. She saw Sharon stand up and kiss Michael on the cheek as she greeted him, but frowned when Sharon saw her standing behind Michael.

"You all remember Vanessa, my wife?" Michael asked as he put his arm around her shoulder.

"Oh—yes, yes, of course," said Sharon, hating the way her words stumbled over each other. Barely able to compose herself, she looked at Vanessa and smiled coyly.

"There's something different about you, Vanessa."

"I am, now that you mention it. I'm pregnant," said Vanessa, her hand rubbing small circles over her bulging stomach.

"No, that's not it." Sharon replied, "I can't quite place it," as she circled her. "Oh, Michael, I got engaged," she said, flaunting her finger, showing a one-carat diamond ring.

"Who's the lucky guy?" Michael asked.

Sharon introduced Dennis, the man sitting between Sheryl and Sherice. Michael shook his hand.

"I'm sure you recognize him," said Sharon. "This is Dennis. He's Mr. Mitchell's son, the owner of Mitchell's Jewelry in Ala Moana."

"Sure, I recognize him from the many advertisements I've seen of him on TV. I heard the Rolex watch ads were a hit."

"You better believe it!" said Sharon.

She then turned to Vanessa as she held up her hand, wiggling her fingers and showing off her engagement ring. Vanessa remained silent and pretended she didn't see it.

Sharon was annoyed Vanessa ignored her. She then said, "Do you want to see my engagement ring, Vanessa? Have you seen such a rock? Dennis is filthy rich. His family owns the leading jewelry store in Honolulu," bragged Sharon.

Vanessa took her hand to check the ring.

"It's lovely," she said, trying not to laugh at a tiny stone like a ring her dad bought for her when she turned twelve as a birthday gift.

Sharon continued to flash her engagement ring, waving it in Vanessa's face as she talked. Vanessa ignored Sharon's childish behavior. She tried hard to control herself and not to say anything rash, but Sharon continued shoving the ring in her face until she couldn't resist it anymore.

"You know, Sharon, your ring looks like what my dad bought for me on my twelfth birthday, but with a bigger stone."

"You are such a kidder, Vanessa. This ring is one-of-a-kind and expensive. What you have is a replica of a Cracker Jack box ring."

Vanessa laughed and shrugged her shoulders when she saw Michael wink at her.

"Yeah, Sharon. That's what it was."

Sharon suggested their tables moved together, so they could talk better. She motioned the server to come over to their table to help them set it up.

"So, what are you guys up to? Vanessa, are you still cleaning those smelly fish? Once we get married, Dennis here will make me an advertising manager in their family business. Isn't that wonderful? It means I'll be making mucho dinero."

"That's terrific, Sharon," said Vanessa.

"I'm glad I didn't end up with Michael. You know, he and I had a thing. Otherwise, I'm stuck on that little island like you: cleaning stinky fish, cooking, and washing clothes. Things little old me can't do. If you are looking for work, Vanessa, I can get you a sales clerk job at the store, but you would have to move to Honolulu."

Vanessa smiled and thanked Sharon for the offer, but she couldn't resist the temptation to ask.

"Sharon, Michael told me you were childhood friends only. Nothing more. Is that right?"

Sharon's face turned red as she changed the subject.

"Hey Michael, I'm inviting you and your wife to my wedding, OK? I can't take no for an answer."

Sharon then turned to Vanessa.

"We're holding it in a banquet room in the new Grandeville Resort, one of the most elegant and well-regarded hotels in the world. Everything is first class. Dennis's rich family will be there. Vanessa, it's a formal attire event. If you have nothing to wear, I am sure I can find something for you in my closet. What size are you? Six? I am size two. Maybe nothing will fit you, you know, with my hourglass figure, but I'm sure I can find something."

"Oh, it's sweet of you, Sharon, but that's OK. I am sure I can find something to wear."

"Are you sure? Formal wear is expensive. I know Michael can't afford it."

"Don't worry, Sharon. I am sure we will manage," Vanessa said.

"Okay, remember, my offer is always open."

Vanessa only smiled and nodded.

Suddenly, the room went silent. A distinguished man and a woman entered the room. Behind them were their bodyguards and a personal secretary.

"Those are the Grandeville's," Dennis whispered to Sharon. "They were at the store yesterday, and I sold Mr. Grandeville a Rolex watch. It was worth over $100,000. He said it was a gift."

"Oh, my gosh! I can't believe I'm dining in the same restaurant as the Grandeville's," whispered Sharon. "This is exciting!"

Tom and Martha looked around the restaurant and smiled when they saw their daughter with Michael. They headed to their table, and Sharon saw them coming toward them.

"Oh, my god, Dennis. They're coming this way to greet you."

"You are right," said Dennis. "I think they recognized me. After all, I gave them excellent service."

To their surprise, as Tom and Martha approached their table, Dennis stood up and shook their hands. The bodyguards tried to stop them, but Tom said it was all right.

"Mr. Grandeville, it is nice to see you again," Dennis said.

Tom had a blank look on his face, but smiled after he recognized him.

"Oh, yeah, Derek, right? From the jewelry store?"

"It's Dennis, sir. And yes, I sold you the Rolex watch, sir."

Tom nodded.

Sharon winked at Vanessa.

"You see? Soon we will rub elbows with the rich and famous."

Vanessa resisted the impulse to laugh. She found Sharon amusing, but had to admit, the night was entertaining.

Moments later, two good-looking guys walked in. Sherice and Sheryl almost had heart attacks. Jason looked handsome wearing jeans and a black shirt, while TJ also wore jeans, but with a striped polo shirt. They looked like male models that came out of a magazine.

"Oh, my god. My future husband just walked in," said Sherice.

"Me, too. My prince charming walked in," said Sheryl. "Oh my god, they're heading this way. They saw me, and they couldn't resist my beauty."

"Shall we order, Vanessa, before it gets crowded? Shopping for a dress is exhausting," Martha said as she kissed her daughter before seating herself next to her.

Sharon felt embarrassed that the Grandeville's hadn't come over to greet Dennis. They came to see Vanessa and thought she must be their personal aide.

"Psst! Vanessa, do you know them? Do you work for the Grandeville's? Why didn't you tell me you already had a job?"

Martha and Tom heard it.

"Work? What does she mean you have a job, Vanessa?" they asked in unison.

"Oh, I'm sorry, ma'am, sir," interrupted Sharon. "I didn't mean for Vanessa to get fired. I thought she was looking for work, and I was just helping her out. I told her we were looking for a sales clerk at the jewelry store where I work. I didn't know she already had a job."

"My daughter works as a salesclerk? Mamma Mia!" said Martha, as if she would pass out.

Sharon swallowed hard, almost fainting.

"D-Did you say your daughter?" she asked apprehensively.

"Yes, she is our only daughter—Vanessa Florence Grandeville," said Tom. "You didn't know she was a Grandeville?"

"And we are her brothers," the twins said simultaneously. "Hi, sis!" said Jason and TJ as they kissed Vanessa and caressed her protruding belly.

Sharon's mouth fell open in disbelief, and she almost fell off her chair. Her face turned red with embarrassment.

"What's for dinner? I'm starving. Where's the food?" Jason asked.

Michael leaned over the table and kissed Vanessa. "I'll check on our food," he said.

Dennis recognized the watch Michael was wearing—the Rolex he sold to Tom Grandeville. He purchased it as a present for his future son-in-law. He bought it for Michael.

Sharon sat for a moment, not knowing what to say. She glanced at Vanessa with a genuine shock.

"I'm sorry. I didn't know," Sharon whispered.

"Don't worry," Vanessa answered.

Moments later, soothing Japanese music played, and everyone moved and swayed back and forth. To Tom and Martha's delight, Michael even helped Akio serve the food. They thought Michael was a down-to-earth person. They looked at their daughter, who was clapping her hands as she watched Michael dance while serving the food, and they could tell how happy she was.

"Who would have thought our daughter, a spoiled brat from birth, would be a kind and caring person? Michael is perfect for her," said Martha, and Tom agreed.

Meanwhile, Sharon could not sit still. Embarrassed by the way she acted, not to mention her attitude toward Vanessa, she didn't know how to make up for it. She saw an opportunity when Vanessa went to the ladies' room. Sharon followed her and apologized for mocking her and begged for her forgiveness.

"Sharon, I forgive you. Jealousy blinded you because Michael ended up with me. You have Dennis now, and I am happy for you."

"Thanks, Vanessa. Friends?" asked Sharon as she stretched her arm to shake her hand.

"Friends," said Vanessa, as they shook hands and then hugged.

As they walked back to their table, Sharon couldn't resist asking Vanessa.

"Is that story you told earlier about the ring your dad gave you and the replica of mine, is that true?"

"No, I was playing you," she answered.

"I thought so," said Sharon, smiling.

"It was a five-carat, not one. My dad bought it from Cartier in New York. I still have it in my room in Beverly Hills. My doll is wearing it. That reminds me. I'll give it to Sophia as a remembrance. I'm sure she'll like that. Don't you think so?"

Sharon fainted.

. . ⌘ . .

IT WAS A LOVELY DAY for a beach wedding. The weather was calm, full of sunlight, with a slight sea breeze. The event planner decorated the dock with garlands, streamers, lanterns, and sparkling lights as they welcomed the guests arriving by boat. There were designated areas for visitors coming by helicopter. Everything was perfect for Vanessa and Michael's nuptials. Despite the rushed preparation, it was a huge affair—a simple wedding with a lavish reception. There were Hula dancers, fire-spitting artists from Honolulu, and a well-known band performing. There were many food and drink options, including American, Asian, Italian, and Hawaiian cuisines.

Vanessa looked radiant in her white lace gown, which was altered because of her protruding belly, as she was five months pregnant on the way. Michael was wearing a plain white linen shirt with a pair of white linen pants. The bridesmaids and flower girl were wearing multi-colored, ruffled, mid-length muumuu dresses. The groomsmen and ring bearer wore multi-colored Hawaiian shirts and white pants. There was a basket of flip-flops where the walkway met the sand, so guests could slip them on and get to their seat without ruining their shoes.

The sound of violins floated in the hushed, fragrant air, and in that calmness, the ceremony began. The flower girl started down the aisle, strewing rose petals as she went, followed by the ring bearer, then the bridesmaids—Jennifer, Stephanie, Alexandra, Samantha, and finally, Rachel—with their groomsmen: Raul, Jason, TJ, Daniel, and Mario. Dr. Fletcher was the best man, and Sophia was the matron of honor.

Vanessa looked like a real princess as she walked down the sandy aisle, with both her father and mother on each side of her. There wasn't a dry eye in the place as they exchanged their vows. It was a lovely ceremony. Soon after that, Michael Simon Angelo and Vanessa Florence Grandeville were finally married.

After the wedding, the new couple had their private party at their favorite place on the beach. Sitting on the trunk of the coconut tree, Michael gazed at Vanessa's swollen abdomen. They smiled together as they felt the baby practice its hourly exercises within her. As the kicks and jabs worked away at her upper belly, Vanessa rubbed the assaulted area, trying to calm her unborn child.

"An active little guy, isn't he? That's my boy!" said Michael as he rubbed her stomach, too.

"You mean the active little girl, right?" Vanessa said as she chuckled.

"Are you guys still at it?" asked Martha. She and Tom had looked for them when they disappeared from the party. "It doesn't matter if it's a boy or a girl. We are so happy that we will be grandparents soon."

"Oh, sorry, Mom! I didn't notice you were there. Michael is too excited about our baby, and at the rate it's kicking me, it will be here in no time," said Vanessa as she let out another chuckle.

"Well, not too early, I hope. You are only five months into the pregnancy. We still have four more months to go. I am in no hurry," said Michael, as he kissed his wife on the lips.

"That's our cue to exit. These lovebirds want to be alone," Tom said as he elbowed his wife.

"I think you are right," Martha said with a grin as she watched Michael rest his head atop Vanessa's. "Loverboy here wants to be romantic with this lovely lady."

Martha and Tom laughed as they left them alone to join the party.

With a soft voice, Michael whispered sweet nothings to Vanessa.

"How about a little snuggle time with your big baby?" said Michael, as he grabbed her hand and walked back to their house.

"Michael, the party, remember? Everyone will look for us."

"Let them look for us. Tonight's our night. We can do anything we want."

"Are you always this persuasive?" she smiled.

"Only for you, my darling, only for you," he smiled back.

Standing in the doorway of their house, and with a beaming grin, Michael swept Vanessa off her feet and carried her across the threshold, catching her off guard. She giggled with delight as she curled up in his arms and laid her head on his chest. A few minutes later, Michael popped a bottle of champagne and poured it into a glass while he poured milk into hers.

The two toasted their glasses together to celebrate their new beginning as husband and wife, and for a night of intimacy. But before going into the bedroom, Michael went to the kitchen, grabbed a piece of paper and a pen, wrote something on it, and taped it to the door. Vanessa waited for him with a smile on her face. Michael grinned, and then he closed the door behind him for a full night of passion and rediscovery.

The guests had a marvelous night dancing to retro seventies and eighties music. Stephanie, Rachel, Alexandra, Samantha, and Jennifer had a good time dancing with Jason, TJ, Raul, Mario, and Daniel. Even Ernesto was having fun dancing with Sophia. Sharon and Dennis joined the conga line, while Sherice and Sheryl were all smiles being serenaded by Hector, Jose, and Alberto. They danced all night, and even Tom's friends and business associates had a great time dancing with the local residents.

It was time to do the traditional bride and groom "money dance" for the guests to express their best wishes with a monetary gift to be donated to the town of Towi Island, but the bride and groom were still missing. Tom and Martha walked to where they last saw them, by the coconut tree trunk, but they were gone.

"Maybe Vanessa got sick, and they went back to their house. Let's see if they are there," said Tom. They walked to the house and were about to knock when Tom saw the note Michael had taped on the door.

"Please do not disturb. Thank you for coming to our wedding. We will see you in the morning at breakfast. Goodnight!"

"Goodness! Don't they ever get tired? She's five months pregnant. It's not like they've never done it before," said Martha after reading the note.

"That son of a gun!" Tom said and put his arm around his wife as they walked back to the party, laughing.

Since the bride and groom were missing, they selected the parents of the bride to do the money dance instead. Standing on the dance floor, everyone danced around Tom and Martha. People were pinning money on their clothes as they danced, and a few threw money at them while Jason and TJ picked it up and placed it in a basket.

Afterward, the lights dimmed, the disco ball rotated with the twinkling lights, and the disco music played all night. The Spoiled Brats Princesses, or SBPs, had everyone busting moves on the dance floor. You could sense their energy mounting as people shouted and danced. The party went on into the early hours. It was an evening of fantastic entertainment and a fabulous time with friends and family.

It had been a long but enjoyable night. Vanessa and Michael's wedding was a memorable night that would live in everyone's memory for many years to come.

EPILOGUE

Towi residents opened their hearts and minds to development and new concepts, and they had tremendous admiration and respect for Michael and Vanessa. Their generosity helped local economy and neighborhood regeneration. They developed tourism and jobs on their island while preserving its rich history, culture, and pride, which they valued.

• • ⚶ • •

TOWI ISLAND'S HISTORY as a fishing village was reflected in a bronze monument of a massive tuna donated by Michael and Vanessa. This statue stood at the port entrance near Towi Island's Visitor Center to provide tourists with a great starting point for exploring the island's beaches and inlets.

The power couple bought the only hotel on Towi Island and constructed the Fisherman's Wife Vacation Resort. They employed anyone who needed work. The resort included all modern amenities, such as Wi-Fi and cable TV in all suites, and free computer access in the mezzanine business areas.

There was The Brats, a mega nightclub with an enormous dance floor, floor-to-ceiling LED displays, local hip-hop DJs, and a high-tech sound system jointly owned by the SBPs, for nightlife-loving guests and partygoers. There was a 24-hour fitness facility for adults and a playground for the youngsters to have fun and play. Individual explorers, couples, and families were immediately drawn to the resort. It was a serene location with fifty big private villas, each with its own terrace facing the lake. There were also dozens of stunning coastal guest rooms. The hotel had an outdoor swimming pool and a water slide for the entire family to enjoy. The hotel lobby had a floral garden and exotic trees and plants. There was a limo service available for their guests on a first come, first serve basis. In addition, a limited supply of bicycles, motorbikes, and mopeds was available for rent at the hotel to tour the island. Those who wish to experience the scenic views while sitting and relaxing may do so for free on an old-fashioned trolley bus.

. . ᴖᴖ . .

FISHERMAN'S WIFE VACATION Resort had an office in Honolulu, and private helicopters or the SuperJet ferry could pick visitors up. There was a park-and-ride parking lot for people to leave their automobiles, because Towi residents still did not allow anyone to bring them onto the island to maintain their quality of life. Michael restored and expanded the docks to accommodate additional vessels. As more people came to Towi Island, he built water and electrical cables. Visitors enjoyed the stunning view of the beach, which included powdery sand that gave the impression they were strolling on a thick carpet. It was the ideal site for surfing, windsurfing, and, of course, fishing.

. . ᴖᴖ . .

MICHAEL REOPENED VANESSA'S old restaurant, modernizing it while keeping the traditional atmosphere. They offered modern comforts like new kitchen appliances and air conditioning. They opened a bicycle and moped rental shop next to their well-stocked mainland food store. There was a souvenir shop with boogie board rentals, beach balls, and new beach gadgets, as well as a bar and a cafe. There was a mid-sized shopping center with over thirty unique shops, such as antique stores, a bookshop, a boutique with clothes and jewelry, a bridal store where Vanessa partnered with her wedding dressmaker, an art museum, and art galleries.

• • ⚜ • •

TOM AND MARTHA ENJOYED the peace and quiet of Towi Island so much that they ditched their fast-paced lives and built a home next to Vanessa and Michael's, being closer to their grandkids. They still attend the board of directors meeting in Los Angeles occasionally. When their parents moved to Towi Island to be full-time grandparents to Vanessa's children, Jason and TJ took over the Grandeville Properties. Once a month, the family would gather on Towi Island or in Los Angeles. They go on a yearly vacation to Asia, Europe, or somewhere close to home.

• • ⚜ • •

THE SUN WAS SOFT AND warm. It was another lovely day on Towi Island. Michael and Vanessa were sitting on their favorite coconut tree trunk on the beach, watching their children play as Michael rubbed her belly. She was eight months pregnant with their third child.

"Who would have thought a simple yet humble fisherman like me would end up with a beautiful, wealthy, and spoiled brat like you?" Michael asked, dabbing the tip of his wife's nose.

Vanessa giggled and kissed her husband. "And who would have believed that a beautiful, rich, and pampered brat like me would ultimately end up with the most precious gift of all—you? Tell me again, when did you fall in love with me?"

Michael gazed at Vanessa in the eyes and pulled her face to his.

"I fell in love with you, Mrs. Vanessa Florence Grandeville-Angelo, the day you almost hit me with your car. It was the best day of my life."

Then Michael took Vanessa's hand in his, and they danced to the beat of their hearts. The spoiled brat and the fisherman lived happily ever after!

· · ❧ · ·

ABOUT THE AUTHOR

.. ~&~ ..

M arissa Marchan writes young adult, new adult, middle grade, and short story fiction for younger readers. Her grandson, Ray Angelo, was the inspiration for *A Ray of Sunshine* and *Ray and Haley in the Kingdom of the Gobtrolls*. It tells the incredible story of a young boy full of love, faith, hope, and courage, filled with heartwarming stories that will lift your spirits and warm your hearts.

Each of us has our own way of expressing our grief and loss. When Marissa's father died many years ago, she discovered she had an incredible ability to create the most wonderful world of pure imagination. She squandered hours fantasizing and making up stories. This was her way of dealing with grief.

Another tragedy struck Marissa's family shortly thereafter, with the death of her sister, Mirla. Marissa struggled with grief and loss for a long time. Ray gave her the strength she needed to move forward. He was a source of love and inspiration for her. Ray instilled in her the courage and ability to persevere in the face of adversity and fear.

Marissa took up writing and could finally put her thoughts into words. Not only did writing help her heal, but it also gave her a sense of stability. She can finally let go.

Since then, Marissa has pursued a writing career, and she is the author of two Spoiled Brats book series: Forbidden Love and Runaway Romance. This series continues with four other novels. A dream she had inspired the character of Mrs. Millionaire, as well as her story.

Read more at https://marissamarchan.com

CONNECT WITH THE AUTHOR

WEBSITE:
Marissamarchan.com[1]
EMAIL:
marissa.marchan@yahoo.com
TWITTER:
@marissamarchan[2]
FACEBOOK:
booksbymarissamarchan[3]
LINKEDIN:
linkedin.com/in/marissa-marchan-41474854[4]
INSTAGRAM:
instagram.com/marissamarchan[5]
PINTEREST
@designbymarissamarchan
TUMBLR
https://marissamarchan.tumblr.com

---

1. http://www.marissamarchan.com/

2. https://twitter.com/marissamarchan

3. https://www.facebook.com/Booksbymarissamarchan/

4. https://www.linkedin.com/in/marissa-marchan-41474854

5. https://www.instagram.com/marissamarchan

MRS. MILLIONAIRE SHORT STORY BOOK SERIES

Mrs. Millionaire Short Story Book series is a collection of fictional stories. Each story focuses on an unlucky family or individual who crosses paths with Mrs. Millionaire.

Matilde "Tilly" Jane Parker begins as a jet setter known for her rebellious streak and reputation as a party girl. When Tilly suffers a personal tragedy, it changes her perspective on life, and her experience has shaped her in many ways. Rather than living her life as a victim, she uses her power and wealth to help those who cannot defend themselves. Tilly finds herself in various situations and occasionally works as an amateur detective who helps people in need solve the problems she is involved in.

MRS. MILLIONAIRE SHORT STORY BOOK SERIES VOLUME 1

.. ❧ ..

Mrs. Millionaire and the Homeless Woman Book 1

∞

MATILDE, OR TILLY TO her family and friends, is well-known for being a party girl. She enjoys unnecessary trouble despite being born into a wealthy family, and her wild behavior worsens as she gets older. Tilly meets Dusty, the man of her dreams, and learns for the first time what it means to give in and when to leave a relationship. But events, even the most uncontrollable and tragic ones, can play tricks on us, change our lives forever, and teach us lessons that we will never forget. Someone attacked Tilly in the underground parking lot, but fortunately a homeless person came by and saved her. That event alters her perspective on life and helps her become a better person.

∞

Mrs. Millionaire and the Bad Father Book 2

∞

Matt Calderon is a caring husband and father of two children. His wife Maria suffers from a condition that limits her ability to perform manual work, forcing Matt to work two jobs to support his family. Despite their difficulties, the family is optimistic. But every now and then life throws a curveball. Matt's boss accused him of stealing money from him. To make matters worse, Matt is in a gas station when a robbery occurs. He is trapped inside, surrounded by police, while his family waits for him to return home. What chances do they have now? Is there hope for them?

Mrs. Millionaire and the Waitress Book 3

∞

Lucy was only two when her mother died. Her father married a widow with two children. Lucy's father never told her the truth about her upbringing, so Lucy assumed her stepmother was her biological mother. Her father died several months before graduating from high school, leaving Lucy with the only family she knew, and they revealed their true colors. Lucy's stepmother secretly transferred her inheritance to herself, and told Lucy that her father had left them penniless. Lucy left school to work as a waitress to support her family. Her stepbrother stole money and valuables from Lucy's work. The owner accused Lucy, and the police arrested her. Will Lucy ever uncover the truth of her past?

∞

Mrs. Millionaire and the Runaway Kids Book 4

∞

After his wife's death, Dexter Curtis accepts a supervisory position at a textile company and moves to Connecticut, determined to provide a better life for his four children. His new job went well, but a colleague was cruel and jealous of him. He ruined Dexter's reputation, resulting in Dexter losing his job. Dexter became depressed after he could not find work and turned to alcohol to relieve his stress. A tragic accident left him unconscious and in a coma. Child Protective Services placed the children in a temporary shelter until they could make other arrangements for them. They wanted to split them into two separate households. The youngsters have escaped because of this chain of events. Will Dexter get out of his coma? Is there a chance to reconcile and mending the family?

Mrs. Millionaire and the Delivery Girl Book 5

∞

The last thing Nancy wanted was to work as a delivery girl. She had high goals in mind. After holding off dating until she got a job, Nancy made it a priority to stay in school and participate in as many activities as possible. Her perception of bad boys and bikers changed when she met Julius. Nancy's ambition to pursue a prosperous career shattered in an instant. They married at City Hall with just a few friends present. Nancy's parents disowned her. When Nancy moved in with Julius's parents in Wisconsin, things turned for the worse. His mother was vengeful and tyrannic. She kept track of every detail of her stay, which irritated Nancy even more. This has caused friction in their relationship. Julius' wandering eye persisted. Nancy discovered her husband was cheating on her and threatened to leave him. Julius begged her not to go. Will Nancy forgive him? Will they continue after the betrayal?

• • ☙ • •

MRS. MILLIONAIRE SHORT STORY BOOK SERIES VOLUME 2

• • ☙ • •

Mrs. Millionaire and the Thief Book 6

∞

HAVE YOU EVER BEEN taken by surprise and had no idea what was going on? To propose to his fiancée, Dan Collins, an advertising account executive, worked hard to get the promotion he wanted. However, a colleague threatens to sabotage his plans for a happily ever after. He sabotages Dan's career, leading to his dismissal, and his life spirals out of control. Will Dan ever prove his innocence? Is a wedding for him still on the horizon?

Mrs. Millionaire and the Housekeeper Book 7

∞

Lesley is a single mother of her seven-year-old daughter Haley. Her boyfriend Stanley disappeared after she gave birth. With nowhere else to go, Lesley makes amends with her mother and returns home. Everything was fine until her mother married Jacob, a man ten years younger, and Lesley's life turned into a massive battleground. Lesley does not get along with him, which leads to friction between her and her mother. Lesley and her daughter moved out of the house after her mother chose her new husband. What will happen to them? Will she be able to support her daughter?

∞

Mrs. Millionaire and the Reluctant Hero Book 8

∞

Ray Griffin is an unfortunate street musician. His wife divorced him and left with their eight-year-old daughter. He has had nothing but bad luck and a series of misfortunes since leaving Texas. Ray became homeless and moved away. He wants to get his life back on track and find a permanent job, so he can regain custody of his daughter. Will Ray overcome the seemingly insurmountable obstacles on his path? Will he see his daughter, whom he has not seen for a long time, and reunite with her?

∞

Mrs. Millionaire and the Elevator Man Book 9

∞

Carlos Angelo, a sixty-two-year-old Italian man, works as an elevator operator in the Lower Manhattan neighborhood of New York City. It was his first and only job in the United States, after nearly four decades in the country. He is known throughout the company as a dedicated, loyal and likeable employee who has received numerous "Employee of the Month" awards over the years. When his employer adapted to new technologies and fired him, he became depressed. What future would he have if he didn't know how to do anything else?

∞

Mrs. Millionaire and the Taxi Driver Book 10

∞

Regie Adams, a forty-year-old dairy farmer, has worked all his life. After several years of feeding, cleaning and milking cows every day, he had had enough and tried his luck elsewhere, despite his mother's protests. Regie boarded a bus outside the city and finds himself in the midst of a series of disasters. Eventually, he found himself in Las Vegas, Nevada. He was content with his simple life as a taxi driver until one fateful night when everything changed. Two men followed a woman who signaled for him to stop. Would this event change his life for the better or for the worse, given his history of bad luck?

SPOILED BRATS BOOK SERIES

The Spoiled Brats Book series is a new adult novel that follows the lives of wealthy teenagers in the affluent city of Beverly Hills. These stories chronicle their extravagant lifestyle, including socializing with the elite and attending private parties, their growth from childhood to maturity, and a serendipitous encounter with love in an unexpected place.

FORBIDDEN LOVE
Spoiled Brats Book Series Book One

• • ∽✠∽ • •

VANESSA FLORENCE GRANDEVILLE, a Beverly Hills socialite and infamous spoiled brat, celebrated her 21st birthday with her wealthy friends in Honolulu. By chance, she ran into Michael, a fisherman from a nearby island, the same day. Vanessa humiliated him, but Michael fell in love at first sight.

Vanessa and her friends had rented a yacht for a weekend cruise when complications arose. Their boat capsized in a fierce storm and swept them overboard. The Coast Guard rescued everyone except Vanessa, who drifted away. Michael found her at sea suffering from a head injury and amnesia. He saved her life, but did he deserve to be regarded as a hero?

Unexpected and remarkable events brought their lives together. Was it possible that life played a joke on them? Will these people overcome their differences?

• • ∽✠∽ • •

RUNAWAY ROMANCE
Spoiled Brats Book Series Book Two

• • ∽✠∽ • •

TWENTY-TWO-YEAR-OLD Beverly Hills socialite Samantha Isabella St. James is devastated when she learns her father intends to force her to marry the son of a wealthy businessman to pay for his debt. She flees on her wedding day and is unaware of the impact of her actions. Samantha seeks refuge in the stranger's house and reluctantly accepts a job as a nanny for Benjamin McClain, an eccentric, handsome young entrepreneur, after someone steals her wallet and leaves her penniless. There is an immediate and clear affinity between them. Will Samantha's life become more complicated when she has to choose between saving her father and following her heart?

A MAGICAL STORYBOOK SERIES

A Magical Storybook Series tells the amazing adventure of a young boy filled with love, faith, hope, and courage, as well as an incredible experience filled with heartwarming stories that will lift your spirits and warm your hearts.

A RAY OF SUNSHINE
A Magical Storybook Series Book One

• • ❧ • •

THEO AND MARY ARE A deformed husband and wife who are constantly mocked in their small town. The townspeople chased them away from the only home they had ever known. With their meager possessions, Theo and Mary travel to the forest, where they discover a magical and mysterious world of beauty and happiness. Soon God blessed them with a child. To Theo and Mary's surprise, he has healing abilities and a connection with the elements and animals. Will Ray's magical abilities be enough to teach the people of the town the true meaning of unconditional love? Can people accept Theo and Mary despite their unappealing appearances? Come along on the adventures of an amazing family, as they use their special abilities to save others and teach people the power of love and understanding.

• • ❧ • •

RAY AND HALEY
In the Kingdom of the Gobtrolls
A Magical Storybook Series Book Two

• • ❧ • •

THEO AND MARY, TOGETHER with their son Ray and daughter Haley, live peacefully and joyfully in an enchanted forest far from civilization. In this strange and mysterious place, Theo and Mary discover that their children were born with unique gifts. Ray possesses extraordinary powers, including the ability to interact with animals and elements, while Haley has a natural ability to communicate with plants and animals. When Theo learns that the people who drove them away from their homes years ago blame them for the desolation of his old town, he must embark on a journey to prove their innocence. When Theo and Haley disappear, Ray uses his wits and magical abilities to find them in the most polluted and smelliest place in the world!

THANK YOU FOR READING!

Thank you for reading *Forbidden Love*. If you enjoyed it, please consider telling your friends or posting a short review. Word of mouth is an author's best friend and much appreciated.

Please check out the rest of Spoiled Brats Book Series, Mrs. Millionaire Short Story Book Series, and A Magical Storybook Series through major online book retailers and distribution channels available as eBooks and Print. Happy reading!

.. ❧ ..

Marissa Marchan

Don't miss out!

Visit the website below and you can sign up to receive emails whenever Marissa Marchan publishes a new book. There's no charge and no obligation.

https://books2read.com/r/B-A-YPEF-UXHIB

BOOKS2READ

Connecting independent readers to independent writers.

Did you love *Forbidden Love: Spoiled Brats Book Series Book One*? Then you should read *Runaway Romance: Spoiled Brats Book Series Book Two*[1] by Marissa Marchan!

Twenty-two-year-old Beverly Hills socialite Samantha Isabella St. James is devastated when she learns her father intends to force her to marry the son of a wealthy businessman as payment for his debt. She flees on her wedding day, completely unaware of the ramifications of her actions. Samantha seeks refuge in the stranger's home and reluctantly accepts employment as a nanny for Benjamin McClain, an eccentric, handsome young entrepreneur, after someone steals her wallet and leaves her

1. https://books2read.com/u/b5Z0A6

2. https://books2read.com/u/b5Z0A6

penniless. There is an instantaneous and clear affinity between them. Will Samantha's life get more complicated when she must choose between saving her father and following her heart?

Read more at www.marissamarchan.com.

About the Publisher

3 Ways Publishing is an independent publisher established in January 2020 to gain recognition and traction in the publishing world.

Do you ever wonder where the idea for your book came from? Was it from a dream? Perhaps a personal experience or story told by your mother or grandmother? Whatever it is, one important thing is that you have to feel passionate about what you write, which leads to a satisfying ending.

3 Ways Publishing publishes books that they are passionate about—books of fictional and entertaining stories to help children develop a love of reading and learning, young readers, fantasy, romance, and fiction for various age groups with a strong female protagonist.

Visit: https://3wayspublishing.com/

www.ingramcontent.com/pod-product-compliance
Lightning Source LLC
Chambersburg PA
CBHW050419260626
47156CB00003B/1070